Boots on the ground

The marines poured out of the Ospreys shouting war cries and hitting the ground running. Some were able to get to positions of concealment on the fringes of the landing zone, but others immediately came under fire from the hidden enemy troops. Men fell where they ran, cut down by bullets that raked their midsections with jagged puncture lines. Others dragged wounded buddies to shell holes or the cover of shattered enemy blockhouses and pillboxes. Still others ran on, engaging the enemy at close quarters with small-arms fire and fixed bayonets.

All over the knob of volcanic rock projecting from the whitecapped seas off the coast of the Philippines, the Marines were landing, taking ground and consolidating their beachheads.

In the first hour of the assault, the lighting-swift coordinated attacks enabled friendly forces to secure an ever-widening cordon of control over the island. As they had done so many times before all over the world, the Marines had come to stay . . .

Titles by David Alexander

SHADOW DOWN

SPECIAL OPS

MARINE FORCE ONE

MARINE FORCE ONE: STRIKE VECTOR

MARINE FORCE ONE: RECON BY FIRE

MARINE FORCE ONE: FROM THE HALLS OF MONTEZUMA

MARINE FORCE ONE

FROM THE HALLS OF MONTEZUMA

David Alexander

BERKLEY BOOKS, NEW YORK

THE BERKLEY PUBLISHING GROUP
Published by the Penguin Group
Penguin Group (USA) Inc.
375 Hudson Street, New York, New York 10014, USA
Penguin Group (Canada), 10 Alcorn Avenue, Toronto, Ontario M4V 3B2, Canada
(a division of Pearson Penguin Canada Inc.)
Penguin Books Ltd., 80 Strand, London WC2R 0RL, England
Penguin Group Ireland, 25 St. Stephen's Green, Dublin 2, Ireland (a division of Penguin Books Ltd.)
Penguin Group (Australia), 250 Camberwell Road, Camberwell, Victoria 3124, Australia
(a division of Pearson Australia Group Pty. Ltd.)
Penguin Books India Pvt. Ltd., 11 Community Centre, Panchsheel Park, New Delhi—110 017, India
Penguin Group (NZ), Cnr. Airborne and Rosedale Roads, Albany, Auckland 1310, New Zealand
(a division of Pearson New Zealand Ltd.)
Penguin Books (South Africa) (Pty.) Ltd., 24 Sturdee Avenue, Rosebank, Johannesburg 2196, South Africa

Penguin Books Ltd., Registered Offices: 80 Strand, London WC2R 0RL, England

FROM THE HALLS OF MONTEZUMA

A Berkley Book / published by arrangement with the author

PRINTING HISTORY
Berkley mass-market edition / April 2005

For information address: The Berkley Publishing Group,
a division of Penguin Group (USA) Inc.,
375 Hudson Street, New York, New York 10014.

ISBN: 0-425-18818-3

BERKLEY®
Berkley Books are published by The Berkley Publishing Group,
a division of Penguin Group (USA) Inc.,
375 Hudson Street, New York, New York 10014.
BERKLEY is a registered trademark of Penguin Group (USA) Inc.
The "B" design is a trademark belonging to Penguin Group (USA) Inc.

PRINTED IN THE UNITED STATES OF AMERICA

10 9 8 7 6 5 4 3 2 1

From the halls of Montezuma,
To the shores of Tripoli,
We fight our country's battles
In the air, on land and sea. . . .

If the Army and the Navy
Ever look on Heaven's scenes,
They will find the streets are guarded
By United States Marines.

—FROM THE MARINE HYMN

Some place-names and descriptions of locales, weaponry, and military procedures have been modified where necessary to suit the requirements of the narrative.

book one:

A Choice of Weapons

"You start to go from the cartels to the cells of terrorists . . . there's a similarity."

—General Shelton, quoted while Chairman of the Joint Chiefs of Staff, 2001.

chapter *one*

Located within the two-hundred-odd miles of wooded territory that encompasses the sprawling Camp Lejeune complex, there is a special forces training facility some call The Dirty Name. The facility is secret and contains the Urban Close-Quarter Battle Range (UCQBR) and Live-Fire Hostage Rescue Training Facility.

Its use is restricted to the brigade known as Marine Force One. Part of the UCQBR contains an accurate mock-up of an urban environment, complete with buildings, signs and billboards of various types, parked vehicles, and motorized dummies located in windows and storefronts. Building materials at the facility are constructed of a concrete-like material that, unlike real concrete, has the ability to absorb small-arms fire at a narrow angle without allowing the bullet to ricochet.

Overseeing the close-quarter battle range is a protected control tower from which it is possible to cause dummies to move about, grenades to detonate, weapons to fire along fixed lines of sight, and to simulate other aspects of an urban combat environment. All of these effects are intended to stress the combat reflexes of special forces personnel to the maximum possible limits.

CCTV cameras monitor every inch of the facility, transmitting real-time video to the control tower, from which supervisory personnel are able to oversee and control every phase of activity taking place down below. The idea behind the UCQBR is to provide trainees with field exercises that duplicate real-world situations as closely as possible.

Creating simulators for tanks, aircraft, marine vessels, and the like is actually easier than doing the same for ground troops, for whom effective simulation must include a wide range of combat conditions in order to be effective. But from ducking and answering retaliatory fire to dealing with simulated hostage situations, Marines undergoing training at the UCQBR complex are given the ability to make mistakes in an environment where such errors are not fatal to themselves or those depending on them.

The scenario that Force One was working on during the team's period of UCQBR simulator qualification time was based on a hypothetical terrorist grab of friendlies encountered in the course of a military operation in a built-up area. It was also an opportunity for Colonel David Saxon, and Sgts. Mainline and Hirsch to get a hands-on feel for the new H&K MP/5-10 SMGs they had just been issued as part of their field kit. Saxon had pushed for the new high-tech SMGs and was gratified to get his pick of the first weapons consignment coming into Lejeune from the H&K plant in Germany.

Almost identical in size and weight to the familiar MP-5 submachine guns familiar to special forces members across the globe, the MP/5-10 SMG fired heavier and more powerful 10mm rounds and had an expanded magazine capacity of sixty-five rounds.

Right now, the three Marine hard-chargers were about to put those weapons to the test as Saxon and Hirsch checked the pull capacity of the climbing ropes secured to their waist at one end and grapnels on the rooftop at the other.

Wearing standard NATO-pattern camo BDUs,

their combat dress included black United Body Armor Equipment TAC-100R tactical face-masks and flak vests, both constructed of Kevlar and both capable of stopping rounds from most handguns, shotguns, and subguns, even at close range.

The flak vests protected their vital areas beneath their camo field jackets. Black fingerless tactical gloves protected hands while leaving fingers free to manipulate the triggers, safeties, and fire-select studs of the H&K SMGs which, for the moment, were slung across their backs.

Linked to both of the other Marines by means of SINCGARS-capable AN/PRC commo and porting a Soviet-made AK-74 Krinov bullpup autorifle, was Sgt. Mainline, positioned in the narrow corridor just outside the flat in which the hostage condition prevailed and one story below the building rooftop on which his partners stood.

"Three. We're in position and proceeding to move," Saxon said into the rice-grain microphone attached to the comset in the "prick" pouch on his load bearings.

"Affirm on that," Sgt. Mainline replied, steadying the short-barreled assault weapon and continuing to keep his eyes glued to the locked door of the flat to which he would be putting the soles of his regulation jump boots in just a few minutes. "I'm good to go." The Krinovs were special-issue to Marine Force One. Saxon had learned their value from long years of familiarity under tough conditions.

"That's affirm. Over."

A moment later, Saxon nodded to Hirsch and both unconventional-warfare specialists began to speed-rappel down opposite walls of the building, paying out the rope with expert precision as they descended from the roof at a speed measured by the pace of their heartbeats.

Quickly they reached their targets: windows set one story down from the roof. The three-way play that went down next happened with blinding speed and lethal efficiency. Faces protected by tactical masks of black Kevlar, Saxon and Hirsch went crashing through the glass panes to target their MP/5-10s on the heads of two terrorist mannequins and take each one of them out in the "tap-tap" style perfected by the SAS—two shots directed either at the head or to the chest—a style which had become the training norm for worldwide counterterror forces from Germany's GSG-9 to the U.S. Delta.

While this was happening, Sgt. Mainline kicked in the door to the flat and went steamrolling into the room on a half-crouch, the Krinov chattering in his fists as he broke sideways to take out the other two terrorist mannequins inside the room. Like Saxon and Hirsch, he had taken down his targets without harming a single hair on a friendlies' head.

"Not bad," Saxon said, checking his Tag-Huer wrist chronometer after hitting the stopwatch function. The entire strike had taken less than four minutes from beginning to end. "But it could have been smoother. Let's take five, then run through it one more time."

Saxon wanted the special-action squad to be in peak readiness for the mission they would undertake in a matter of days. Despite back-channel diplomatic efforts, the weapons depot in France still contained crates of maraging steel for the Father Colonel's latest nuclear weapons project. Saxon's team would insure that the technology never left the Marseilles docks.

Three days later, Saxon and his people deployed into the operations zone on three separate commercial flights. These flights originated from as many different departure points in the United States and in Europe. All Force One personnel reached Marseilles International Airport within a few hours of each others' arrivals.

The Marines were checked through customs without incident, bearing flash I.D. supplied by

One's CIA-run intelligence support activity, codenamed Yellow Light. But in the case of unit commander David Saxon, not all went as smoothly as it might have appeared.

While Mainline and Hirsch passed through customs undetected, a sharp-eyed airport security agent monitored arrivals on screens hardwired to security cams and linked to a face-matching database that had been set up to spot watch-listed individuals. He identified the new arrival as someone of whom to take special note.

All governments compiled watch lists of those who, for a variety of political and operational reasons, were deemed of importance and bore close scrutiny. David Saxon, due to his covert activities throughout the years, was one of these aforementioned individuals. The security agent at Marseilles International recognized the face beneath the soft felt hat and punched up a still from the videotape feed coming off the CCTV cameras. Biometric matching turned up a close similarity between it and Saxon, one that was close enough for the security agent to read as a confirm.

But the confirm was never reported. Not to the arm of the French Ministry of Defense, the *Group d'Intervention de la Gendarmerie Nationale* or GIGN, which is responsible for that nation's counterterror activities and internal security arrangements. The security agent, originally a native of Algeria, was secretly working for the Libyan Mukhabarat, or Secret Intelligence Service, and he had recently received instructions from his case officer to attach priority importance to sightings of any known U.S. intelligence personnel passing through his surveillance station.

This he did at a dead-drop during a lunch break only an hour after the sighting.

On arrival via diplomatic pouch, the raw intelligence was analyzed in Tripoli a little while later. Soon the finished intelligence product was being passed to the Iranians, who dispatched a shooter team to France comprising members of an Al Qadr terrorist offshoot, the Iranian Party of the Faithful.

chapter *two*

While final preparations were being made to bring the shooters into France (a process that would involve circuitous travel arrangements, since the French GIGN would move swiftly against such operatives if they were sighted), Saxon's team had arrived separately at a safe house in the St. Antoine district, maintained by the CIA and overseen by One's spook liaison, Rempt.

Doc Jeckyll, One's technical and communications officer, was gratified to find that the intelligence satellite downlink equipment was in good order and functioned correctly. He immediately seated himself at the console of screens and began punching in coded sequences which would put him in touch with an Improved Crystal Two phased satellite array located approximately one hundred fifty thousand feet above the earth in a low orbit.

While Jeckyll busied himself at the computer equipment, Saxon, Hirsch, and Mainline inspected the military ordnance that had been requisitioned for the strike.

The equipment manifest tallied with the hardware on-site.

Three carrying-cases with Heckler-Koch MP/5-10 submachine guns nestled in their die-cut foam interiors were waiting for the team, as were several hundred rounds of 10mm ammo for the guns and spare ABS plastic magazines.

The ammunition came in two forms: green tracers and standard full-metal jacketed hardball.

Hush Puppy–type silencers that were custom-threaded for each weapon by CIA armor artificers were also included in the package to afford One with the capability to inflict whispering death on the opposition.

Considerations leading to the One team having selected the H&Ks for the mission above the AK-74 Krinovs, which were its usual weapons of choice, were twofold.

Firstly, there were special field requirements, dictated by the trade-off between firepower and concealability, for which the H&K SMG appeared to be the best choice, hands down.

Secondly, the mission parameters would call for close-quarter fighting, for which the MP/5-10 SMGs had a small but decisive tactical edge over the bullpup Russian rifles for the specific mission requirements.

But as far as personal sidearms went, the Sig-Sauer P228 9mm semiautomatic pistols favored by One would continue to be standard armament on this current search-and-destroy run. The compact Sigs—outfitted with the currently fashionable New York trigger—were concealable, controllable, and had the stopping power of large-frame handguns.

As was the case with the MP/5-10s, there were several hundred rounds of ammunition apiece as well as spare magazines for the Sigs, which, however, were expanding-head-type as opposed to hardball.

Battle dress for the mission was also provided for the team. This included NATO-standard camouflage BDUs, Kevlar tactical vests, tactical face masks, and load-bearing suspenders. The load bearings were equipped with mag and radio pouches for the compact SINCGARS-capable AN/PRC-4000 communicator units (the latter equipped with constrictor straps), which had served One well on previous strikes, and which they would now again take with them into the field along with the UM84 Universal Military Holster for the P228s.

In addition, there were miscellaneous items provided for One as well. The list included Cyalume lightsticks; climbing tackle; APERS, FRAG, and STUN grenades; and the battle-tested KA-BAR combat knives, which were preferred by each member of the One team above more modern designs, such as those by Ek, due to their proven reliability and feel in the hand.

Having carefully gone over the equipment manifest, Saxon, Mainline, and Hirsch gave their attention to Doc Jeckyll. Seated at a console bearing several high-definition computer screens, he had patched into the Improved Crystal satellite array and now had a secure downlink directly from the PHOTINT spysat's orbital perspective.

This encoded transmission was converted into a real-time high-resolution graphic display by the overclocked image-processing architecture of the proprietary computer hardware. The system deployed had been custom-designed decades before by the late Seymour Cray specifically for use in the field and was still considered beyond then-current technological limitations. It had taken a while for technology to catch up with Cray's inventive mind.

Some called this secure remote imaging system the keystone of his career. It was rumored that Cray had devoted so much attention toward making the system state-of-the-art that the Cray Computer company had delayed a supercomputer delivery to the Lawrence Livermore Laboratories, a thirty million dollar loss that had been made up by the CIA out of covert imprest funds.

The twenty-four-inch flat-panel screen to which Saxon, Hirsch, and Mainline devoted their attention was a top-down view of one of the islands lying just off the coast of Marseilles. A sidebar identified this particular spit of land in the Mediterranean as Chat Noir—Black Cat.

"Note the fortifications," Jeckyll said to his buddies, highlighting the terrain feature he was pointing out with a mouse cursor in the shape of an arrow. "These cylindrical structures here in the upper left are gun emplacements. I make them as Norinco Type-75 or 75-1, 14.5 millimeter triple-a guns. The one on the right could be an Oberlikon, but I'm not sure yet."

"Looks like troop barracks, too," Saxon put in,

noting a series of oblong features over on the right of the satellite photo.

"Good guess," Jeckyll put in. "That's probably right—ballpark-wise, anyway."

Before the high-resolution PHOTINT satellite completed its transit over the target, Jeckyll had pointed out a number of other features, both natural and manmade on the island that would prove either useful or detrimental to an assault force. All would be taken into account during the final planning phase of the mission.

At 0349 hours (Zulu), Saxon and the two other members of the One buddy team prepared to converge on the target. They were outfitted with camouflage BDUs from which ordnance and other combat material was festooned on their load-bearing suspenders. Their combat dress included Fritz helmets optionally equipped with ghillie cover. Tactical face masks were also part of the field kit.

Equipment to be utilized on the strike included small footprint communications apparatus. As had been the case during previous covert search-and-destroy field operations, AN/PRC-4000 comsets were carried high on each One ground asset's chest in radio pouches, placing the "pricks" within easy reach.

The Heckler-Koch MP/5-10 SMGs that One had gained proficiency on at Lejeune's UCQBR during the strike team's grueling series of qual-sim exercises prior to being mobilized for the mission now rode their backs on combat slings as One prepared to deploy on its target.

This was a fortified villa that lay beyond the heights of the island's coast. The sprawling estate had been defensively augmented. In addition, new structures and earthworks had recently been added to the compound. About thirty yards beyond the wave-tossed beach of the southern French coastline to which they had deployed to await the arrival of support infrastructure personnel, the Marines spotted the infrared strobe marking the position of the trawling vessel that the One raiding detail had been expecting.

Invisible to the naked eye, the IR strobe was readily discernible to One thanks to the AN/PVS night vision goggles (NVGs) they wore. These sophisticated items of night observation field equipment were outfitted with GEN IV image-intensification tubes, highly resistant to bloom-out and offering excellent resolution.

Saxon's people replied with a signal strobe of their own and deployed to the beach zone. Once the skipper of the vessel exchanged verbal recognition codes with Saxon and his men—who kept their weapons trained on him until he had done so, a necessity dictated by proper fieldcraft procedures—they boarded the boat, which, despite its ramshackle appearance, was powered by a 1,000-horsepower Mercruiser engine.

The skipper was a CIA contract operative who came from a long line of those doing jobs for the Company in furtherance of their political beliefs. His grandfather had been a member of a French partisan network, who during World War II had assisted the legendary Jedburgh teams of the OSS, and he himself had participated in several covert ops during the Cold War years. Besides the engine, the boat was equipped with a few other nonstandard high-tech features as well, including sophisticated radar and sonar gear and long-range, satellite-capable communications equipment.

But the most surprising nonstandard feature of the vessel was the cargo that it carried concealed under a tarp on its afterdeck. This was a versatile craft known as a subskimmer. The subskimmer was originally developed by the British for use by the

SBS, or Special Boat Services, their equivalent of the U.S. Navy's SEALs. Designed to carry out waterborne commando assault-style missions, the rigid-hull inflatable craft powered by its ninety-HP outboard engine is both a fast surface vessel and a stealthy, submersible, driven when fully submerged by two battery-enabled electric motors.

The skipper of the trawling vessel knew what was expected of him. He was to bring the boat out to within a kilometer of the Chat Noir shoreline and then drop anchor. While the subskimmers were capable of shuttling One the entire distance from shore, it was deemed advisable from a tactical standpoint to have the team deploy from the ocean under cover of darkness.

The American commando raiders onboard would then proceed the rest of the way underwater, RVing with the boat on completion of the mission. While the trawler chugged through the moonless night, Saxon, Mainline, and Hirsch occupied themselves by climbing into their wetsuits and strapping the supplied CCR-25 closed-circuit oxygen SCUBA gear onto their backs.

Designed for long-duration, shallow-depth military diving, the CCR-25 rebreathers functioned by scrubbing CO_2 from recycled air through advanced-design chemical filters and did not leave behind a trail of bubbles as was the case with conventional SCUBA tanks.

Permitting dives up to three hours in duration, the units were well-suited to facilitate stealthy incursion activities in pursuit of covert strike objectives.

When the skipper of the trawler told Saxon and company that the boat was in position just over a hundred meters beyond the island in the dark seas, he assisted them in lowering the subskimmer over the side of the vessel with a cable winch.

As the delivery craft was being lowered away, the subskimmer's front flotation bladder was pumped full of compressed air to keep the bow from dipping and also to stabilize the craft.

Once the vessel was in the water, the three One bangers went over the side of the boat and seated themselves inside the subskimmer. The skipper of the vessel watched the covert delivery craft submerge as the front bladder was deflated and its buoyancy box was partially voided to establish a negative buoyancy. It soon vanished from sight beneath the surface of the ink-black waters.

Moments later there was not a single trace of the commando team. With a brief glance at the dark hulk of Black Cat Island in the near distance, the skipper turned and went back into the wheelhouse. His role in the mission complete, at least for the present, he raised anchor and began to chug from the drop zone.

chapter *three*

With Sgt. Berlin' Hirsch behind the handlebar controls of the submersible vessel, the sub-skimmer glided beneath the waters of the Mediterranean like some hydra-headed sea beast. Its specially silenced engine and the rebreather gear One wore combined to make the commando raider unit's progress utterly stealthy.

In a short while the Marines—navigating by means of submersible underwater night-vision goggles (UNVGs), which incorporated an infrared source for improved visibility under poor ambient light conditions—had negotiated the marine environment and had reached the vicinity of Black Cat Island.

There they had already scouted out a protected hide site for the subskimmer by carefully analyzing the high-grade satellite visuals that had been beamed down from the Improved Crystal Two spy platforms in low-trajectory earth orbit. The hide site selected was a small marine cove from which the beach zone could be quickly acquired by climbing a gently upsloping, though rocky rise. Still keeping the subskimmer submerged, Hirsch jockeyed the nimble little craft into the cove, then he forced air into its buoyancy box from the amphibious unit's compressed air tanks.

The subskimmer broke the surface of the water like a many-headed sea creature rising in the night as its flotation bladders next filled with compressed air. Making it fast by hawser lines to nearby rocks, the three commandos removed their SCUBA gear and, garbed in the camo BDUs they had worn underneath their suits, waded in the shallow water toward the rocky beach of Black Cat Island.

While Saxon and Mainline kept guard, now scanning the shoreline through standard, non-immersible NVGs and keeping the H&K MP/5-10 SMGs ready to engage hostiles should any appear, Hirsch took the point, making for the heights. Signaling the all-clear, Hirsch saw Saxon and Mainline make to follow him through the electronic view field of his NVGs.

Within a matter of seconds all three One personnel were in place on the ground. They were now deployed in depth to perform their preliminary recce of the strike perimeter. As they stole across the windswept landscape, they saw the strike zone through their flickering electronic eyes.

The aggressor team was on site and mobile.

One owned the night.

Saxon, Mainline, and Hirsch each stealthily deployed to three preplanned strike sectors on the perimeter of the warehouse entrepot—code-named Amber, Blue, and Chrome, respectively. Keeping their profiles low and trusting in the pattern-breaking properties of their BDUs' NATO camo pattern to do the rest in rendering them invisible in the indigo blackness, each member of the One team scanned their individual sector through their AN/PVS fourth-generation night vision goggles.

From his position of concealment behind a jumble of black basaltic boulders wrenched from the sea in some ancient volcanic upheaval, David Saxon kept his MP/5-10 in front of him as he lay doggo and swept his glance back and forth in a practiced scanning pattern.

His sector appeared to be much in the state of readiness that he had expected it to be. There was one guard walking his perimeter. The sentry was not equipped with NVGs and carried an FN/FAL long-barreled rifle variant—a common firearm in this part of the world, in some respects more so than the ubiquitous *Kalashnikova Avtomats* and their numerous derivatives.

While Saxon continued his prestrike sector scan, Sgt. Mainline was performing similar recce operations on his end of the mission. The shimmering false-color video view field of Mainline's NVGs revealed that his own sector was ripe for a strike. Berlin' Hirsch was in position as well, training the Litton image intensification scope of his MP/5-10 on the sentry in the guard tower overhead, having pushed his NVGs up on his sweat rag.

The security crow's nest was some thirty meters in height. When the sentry within its confines was perfectly framed between the white cross reticules of the starlight scope, Hirsch took a deep breath and squeezed off a sound-suppressed 9mm round.

He watched as the asset in the crow's nest pitched backward from the impact of the single round, which had penetrated the left quadrant of his torso and punctured his heart. A spray of blood marked the single entrance wound as ballistic energy transfer of the impacting round caused massive internal damage to cardiac and pulmonary tissue.

A moment later, Saxon heard the three radio clicks signaling that Hirsch, in position at Chrome, had taken out the opposition resource in the crow's nest and was deploying into the target strike perimeter. Saxon heard the two answering clicks, which signaled to him that Mainline was moving as well on Blue.

Saxon reached toward the AN/PRC-4000 nestled in its Velcro pouch on the load-bearing suspenders he wore and depressed the comset's talk button once, sending his own confirmation to Mainline and Hirsch. Then, his weapon held at the ready, Saxon broke from his position toward Amber, negotiating the windswept ground on a low, fast trot.

Two 10mm bursts from the MP/5-10 in Saxon's tactical-gloved hands dropped the sentry in his tracks. Wearing khaki fatigues, the perimeter walker had been on his patrol when Saxon jumped down from the top of the fence directly behind him. The opposition player had spun around at the sound behind him and brought his weapon up from the muzzle-down position in which he had been porting it while walking his night watch.

Saxon had already acquired his man with the MP/5-10. In such a tactical situation it was the combatant that got the drop on his opponent who usually walked away instead of being dragged away. The sound-suppressed bursts exited the mouth of the SMG's Hush Puppy–type muzzle attachment with barely a whisper, punching through the sentry's heart region and inducing massive physical trauma resulting in the aspiration of large amounts of dark aortal blood.

Collapsing, the terminated asset dropped to the dirt and Saxon dragged him quickly from sight, concealing the takedown in the shadowy recesses just within the perimeter enclosure that ran around the base compound. Precision-coordinated with Saxon's lethal actions, Hirsch and Mainline were taking down their targets as well at Blue and Chrome sectors elsewhere on the strike-site perimeter.

The targets were terminated swiftly and silently, much in the same manner as those sentries that Saxon had taken out at his end of the op, and these too were stashed where they were likely to remain hidden for some time to come.

Having dispatched their designated targets, Saxon,

Hirsch, and Mainline proceeded to carry out the second assigned phase of the base penetration. During this secondary phase, each member of the covert warfare specialist unit would deploy to their preselected demolition sites and emplace timed high-explosive munitions packages containing the high-blast-yield compound, Octol.

On completion of their assigned tasks, the strike force would extract singly from the target area and withdraw to the rally point on the beach zone.

Saxon's assigned demolition site was the storage facility itself. Reaching this priority target by loping stealthily through the shadows of the base, the One honcho was not surprised by signs of activity he encountered at the site—a low-rise building of cinderblock with a slab roof.

As he covertly scanned the combat environment through NVGs, a four-by-four that had come in through the villa's main gates pulled up and three men got out. These individuals promptly vanished inside the transshipment area. He could not be completely certain, but Saxon thought he recognized Hans Rohlfing and Chivu Mihalescu among them, two key assets intel had linked to the weapons smuggling activities on Chat Noir.

Saxon waited until they were out of sight and unshipped the munitions he'd brought along.

Removing the circular, black general-purpose mines—each containing six kilograms of Octol-based plastic explosive—Saxon slotted the demo charges at critical points along the exterior of the building.

They were so emplaced so that the force of the blast would hurl the walls inward when the explosives detonated, resulting in maximum structural damage to the designated architectural target site. Although the charges all were enabled with radio-linked backup capable of initializing detonation by manual activation should operational contingencies require it, timed explosion was the selected primary method of ignition.

To facilitate this pyrotechnic event, Saxon inserted a detonator into each mine. The electrically actuated detonators were wired to a Bressel digital fuse programmer. The detonators incorporated a built-in fail-safe feature that would trigger the lethal submunitions if they were moved or otherwise tampered with after emplacement.

Setting the timers on the demolition mines for twelve-minute delays, Saxon moved at speed toward his pre-assigned extraction point. By this point Hirsch and Mainline had completed their assigned mission roles as well. Hirsch had taken longer, due to the necessity of taking down the sentry who was guarding the base arms depot.

Shooting the sentry in the face at close range with the MP/5-10, Hirsch quickly neutralized the lock on the steel door using a torque hammer device and was soon inside. The charges slotted, he was out again in just under six minutes.

Mainline's assigned demolition site had been the barracks buildings housing the island fortress' rank-and-file personnel. He had drawn this assignment principally because he was practiced at taking these structures down—adept at crawling under, around, and through populated areas without being heard, seen, or otherwise detected.

Sliding into the crawl space between the cool dirt and the wooden floor of the building, Mainline slotted his demo charges, hearing the sounds of footfalls over his head as he set the last of the detonators with the Bressel digital fuse programmer on the general-purpose mines.

Having completed his tasks, Mainline proceeded with stealth through the darkness of the compound toward his assigned extraction point, alternating fast sprints with sudden halts to scan for assets conducting countersurveillance activity. By this time, Saxon had already reached his extraction point and was tugging on the nylon climbing rope that was anchored to the top of the wall by a steel grapnel.

Ascending the wall, Saxon rappelled down the other side barely a scant few minutes ahead of One's two other hard-chargers who were performing similar actions in their sectors. In a matter of minutes the three Marines had come and gone like shadows in the night. Unseen and unknown, they had primed the base for the maximum level of exploitation.

Standing to at the rally point, Saxon consulted his wrist chronometer and pressed the stud that illuminated the dial with infrared light undetectable to the unaided eye but readily visible through the AN/PVS NVGs he wore.

The line of digits informed Saxon that it was just over three minutes toward detonation of the mines. Hirsch and Mainline had better hustle.

Following in just under a minute later, the two covert warfare specialists had rejoined the team leader at rally point Donkey. Saxon, Mainline, and Hirsch hunkered behind the protection of the jumble of basaltic boulders just above the cove where the subskimmer was moored, and Saxon unshipped the remote-fire control unit to be used just in case the timers did not trigger the munitions while consulting his chronometer.

Like Saxon, Mainline and Hirsch had removed the night-vision goggles that had been worn during their stealth strike, blinking away the lingering after-effects of prolonged exposure to NVGs. This took the form of after-images which usually required several minutes to fade completely from the view field.

The countdown toward detonation continued until only a line of zeros remained on the face of Saxon's watch.

A pulse-beat after the time had maxed out, Saxon realized that the remote backup would not be necessary as a blinding, white incandescence lit up the horizon, exposing the terrain features of Black Cat Island that had been hidden from view under cover of darkness.

Despite the advanced anti-bloom features of the GEN-IV NVGs, the strike team would have been blinded by the light of the blast had they been wearing their image-intensification goggles during the explosion. The thunderclap of the primary charges exploding in perfect synchronization came a fraction of a second later, traveling far slower than the light generated by the blast, but faster than the wave front generated by concussive effect, which arrived a heartbeat after the sound of the explosion.

As they watched the entire base go up in a ballooning mass of flame, noise, and smoke, Saxon,

Mainline, and Hirsch felt the searing heat and blast effect finally reaching them as they turned and scrambled down the incline toward the cove with Hirsch in the lead and Saxon covering their retreat at the rear of the three-man column.

Minutes after getting onboard the subskimmer, the three Marines had once again climbed into their rebreather-equipped SCUBA suits.

While Saxon and Mainline pushed the subskimmer out of the cove and into open water, Hirsch was putting the delivery craft into a dive. Once fully submerged, the team proceeded the rest of the distance underwater until they detected the flash of the infrared strobe positioned on the trawler's port bow through submersible UNVGs.

The skipper helped them aboard, and they watched the last fires of the destroyed base on Black Cat Island as he set course for the mainland and pulled out the throttle to begin the short trip back.

book two:

A Frontline Objective

"In modern mobile warfare the tactics are not the main thing. The decisive factor is the organization of one's resources—to maintain the momentum."

—General Ludwig von Thona,
Rommel's Afrika Korps.

chapter *four*

Amazonia. Attack Sector Bravo.

The chopper sortie flew in a star-shaped echelon no more than thirty feet above the tops of the tallest trees. This made it vulnerable to shoulder-launched SAMs and even small arms fire, but that couldn't be helped.

The helos had orbited the hot LZ while Marine Super Cobras suppressed enemy fire down in the jungle. The word had just come down over the comms net that the LZ was cleared for landing. This didn't mean a hell of a lot. Just one bad actor down there with an RPG or a Strela launcher balanced on his shoulder could do a motherload of damage.

The choppers approached the LZ, which was not marked with smoke but showed up on control screens on instrument consoles, giving the helo jocks downlinked GPS position data on a moving map display.

The helos settled down but didn't touch their undersurfaces to the earth. They kept their main rotors dishing at high rotational speeds while the troops jumped out and hit the LZ running like fiends. The second that the last Marine was unassed, they soared straight up and got the hell out of there.

Anybody would have.

This was bandit country, and the jungle was full of the Evangelist's guerilla partisans.

Carlos Evangelista studied the skies. The Evangelist smiled. It was not a pleasant thing to see. His men had seen such smiles before. They themselves did not smile but kept their faces set gravely as they stood by and watched.

The captive, an American soldier, was tied to the tree trunk. She was naked. A dog collar had been fastened around her neck. She had not been molested as men might molest a woman, but as men might molest other men in order to humiliate them before questioning or execution. There was, after all, a time to rape and a time to kill.

Now was the time to kill.

This is why the Evangelist was smiling his unpleasant smile and why his men were silent and as grave as a village priest presiding at a peasant funeral.

Evangelista said a prayer to his knife. Behind him in a semicircle his assembled partisans waited to view the execution of the captured American soldier. It was not long in coming. His prayer completed, Evangelista kissed the blade of his knife and grabbed the captive by the hair. She was *una rubia,* a blonde one; he liked them this way.

Then, with one swift lunge of the blade across the naked throat the head was nearly severed, the killing done. Another stroke in the opposite direction, through hot, spurting blood, severed it completely. The Evangelist grabbed the grim trophy by the hair, noting with satisfaction that the eyes still blinked and the mouth still moved, and held it aloft, both a trophy of battle and an augury of coming victory to the cause.

The assemblage cheered their leader. More, they wanted. *Otro mas!* some chanted. *Venceremos!* shouted others. He would give them more. Plenty of it. Soon for the first. For those others who clamored for final victory, the wait would be a little longer. But it, too, would come in the end.

The second captive, also an American soldier, was now ready to die. The executioner looked at El Jefe with expectation. The partisan had been chosen from among the guerilleros to execute this second *yanqui cabron*. He held the machete poised to strike. Its well-honed blade gleamed brightly. The Evangelist, stained with fresh blood from the killing of his own sacrifice to *la causa*, nodded. The executioner drew back his arm and prepared to strike off the American soldier's head.

The ground suddenly shook.

Blast waves and flames engulfed the clearing as the rocket strike commenced. The salvo lit up the crude huts and barracks longhouses surrounding the clearing where the executions had been taking place. Shrapnel cooking off a warhead tore through the executioner, flaying him alive. A severed forearm with a hand still clutching the hilt of the blood-dripping machete went flipping into the mud. The captive who had minutes before been within an ace of meeting his maker unchained himself. He took one final look at the headless soldier and ran into the jungle.

He ran until he saw the helo weave back across the encircling tree line clearing. He waved his arms.

The helo made an axial thirty-degree turn and began to descend. As it reached the chest level of the partisans' former captive, strong hands pulled him inside.

"What the fuck kept you assholes?" he asked.

The troops in the chopper understood: They were all Marines.

The CH-130-H Hercules transited off the runway and angled up at the sky, going wheels-up.

The island sat like a toad on a lily pad off the western coast of Brazil. Morning sunlight gleamed off the reflective surfaces on the flight deck, throwing off spokes and glimmers at strange and constantly shifting angles.

It was 0912 hours (Lima). The flight deck had developed a noticeably musty smell. This tended to happen in these southern latitudes.

The prop-driven transport aircraft climbed to twenty thousand feet and leveled off, its four engines reducing to a low growl as the pilot throttled down to cut speed. Navigating by GPS, the pilot set course for the first waypoint of the flight.

The Hercules swung right and lumbered inland, buffeted by thermals coming off the surface of the sea. It was soon over the coastline and gliding across the scrub jungle below. The pilot set course for the second and last waypoint of the journey, from runway to initial point.

Over the aircraft's interphone he told the loadmaster to get ready to do his thing.

Yanqui Big Thunder was all set to boom.

Duke's Castle. Force One's operating location was situated at FOL Mantra, a stretch of jungle in the middle of nowhere that had recently become an extension of the USA.

Mantra had been selected because it was located near Amazonia Attack Sector Bravo and because the Brazilian government had permitted the U.S. to lease it for military use for the next six months, renewable under easy payment terms. Technically, it was an FOL, a forward operational location. Informally, the legs called it a "rent-a-base" when they weren't calling it less pleasant things.

Duke's Castle was a cleared circle in the midst of double-canopy jungle. Its security perimeter was surrounded by a circular ditch and an extensive system of earthworks and sandbag barricades. Guard towers rose at four corners above these and a ten-foot-high security fence.

In the interior of the camp, rows of Quonset huts and low-rise cinder-block structures suggested command posts and troop barracks. Here also there were revetments for mobile armor and landing areas large enough to accommodate helicopters or VSTOL aircraft, such as the naval variants of the F-35 Joint Strike Fighters flown by Marine aviation to replace the venerable Harriers of the twentieth century.

Outwardly, forward operations location Mantra resembled a firebase from out of the Vietnam conflict. Appearances can be deceiving, though, and this was the case with this FOL.

Most of Duke's Castle had been built underground using a cut-and-cover system for speedy construction of command bunkers, like the kind used to build the New York City subway. Essentially, a big hole was dug, the sides reinforced by steel and concrete, cushioned against shock by enormous coiled springs, and then prefab steel cubes were lowered in by crane. The boxes of hardened steel and concrete were cushioned from blast by massive shock absorbers. Breathable air was recirculated and scrubbed of contaminants and impurities.

Secure command, control, communications, computing, and intelligence, surveillance, and reconnaissance (C^4ISR) links extended the tactical vision of Duke's Castle to straddle the globe. Network-centric warfare meant that Duke's Castle was a node on an invisible chain of command centers networked into a grid of C^{4}ISR assets on land, sea, and air. The enemy used stealth to leverage its far more poorly equipped and organized forces, but the government forces also had stealth on its side.

The main operational focus was to clear the sector of guerilla activity. Attack Sector Bravo teemed with insurrectionist forces. That was Detachment Delta's primary mission.

The detachment was a battalion-strength force hived off from the Marine Force One brigade. The battalion was further split into company-strength elements optimized for land mobile operations.

Delta had been launching fire recons into Amazonia for the last three weeks to gather tactical intelligence, pinpoint targets, and perform battle damage assessments. Snatch-and-grab missions had hauled in captives who had spilled information concerning the partisans' operational plans, patrol habits, and other useful strike data.

Today marked the commencement of operation Big Thunder. The op had been planned for months. The OPLAN called for mobile teams working under a joint unified tasking command to search out and destroy partisan encampments, weapons dumps, and staging areas deep in the five-hundred-mile expanse of jungle known as Amazonia Attack Sector Bravo.

Lieutenant Bart "Doc" Jeckyll watched the real-time false-color video feed through the view field of a lightweight head-mounted display.

From thirty thousand feet in the air, the image resolved itself into a recognizable panorama of double canopy jungle far below. Marine Force One's chief technical clicked on the map overlay to further clarify the image that floated in front of his eyes. The overlay showed a map of southwestern Brazil. A blue rectangle that encompassed a swath of territory as large as Rhode Island showed the articulated branches of river tributaries like capillaries extending outward from a massive vein.

Jeckyll blinked to click on a smaller box displaying the flight path of the UCAV to which he was uplinked. The wire grid diagram in red and blue indicated that the unmanned combat aerial vehicle was still a thousand miles slant range of the designated target.

The Doc switched screens to check the progress of another remote robotic weapon system. The new display showed the interior of a tunnel. The crawling robot had inserted itself into a bunker complex bored into the side of a mountain. The robot had stealthily evaded all of the base's perimeter defenses.

It was now transmitting real-time video, live audio, and chemical-biological weapons analysis from sniffed samples of ambient air to Jeckyll's monitoring equipment back at Duke's Castle, where Jeckyll had a Quonset hut crammed with gear that was his and nobody else's to play with.

Not even One's commander, David Saxon, could play in the Doc's techno-sandbox unless he was invited. Saxon was waiting for Jeckyll's report, though. Elsewhere in the underground installation Saxon was at the moment meeting with a planning cell for another mission. Jeckyll switched displays again and now studied the real-time feed from a third of the nasty surprises for the enemy that he had deployed robotically across the length and breadth of Attack Sector Bravo.

Lt. Col. David Saxon was a square-jawed man with close-cropped hair whose face rarely changed expression, except when he smiled, which wasn't all that often. Saxon, commander of Marine Force One, sat at a trestle table on whose top was scattered an assortment of computer and communications gear and faced the flat-panel display screen high on the opposite wall of the underground bunker.

The screen connected him to a secure room in the National Military Command Center (NMCC) at the Pentagon, to the National Security Council (NSC) meeting room beneath the Oval Office at the White House, and also—unusually—to the office of the Secretary of Defense's fourth-floor E-Ring office directly above the Pentagon's River Entrance facing the western bank of the Potomac River.

It was uncharacteristic for the SecDef to take an active part in mission briefs as it was the deputies of department honchos who generally ran the show at the operational level. The chiefs traditionally set policy and briefed the president and the press. The deputies performed the stubby-pencil work that made wheels turn.

It was now the deputies who were seated around the NSC crisis room's square oak table with their sub-chiefs or "backseaters" filling most of the available seating ranged along the north wall of the not-very-large room. Defense Secretary Warren Hunnicut's presence on the net today, although largely ceremonial, reflected the importance of Operation Big Thunder.

Later, the president would use his nationally televised State of the Union address to inform the nation of the events in South and Central America, largely based on Hunnicut's report. Once the SecDef had completed his brief to commanders in the field, he would board his limo and ride across the 15th Street Bridge into the District.

Admitted into the White House via the West Wing entrance, Hunnicut would brief the president as part of the "Seven Dwarves"—President Travis Claymore's privileged inner circle. It was made up of the president's closest and most trusted personal advisers, and as such was distinct from the normal presidential cabinet, which, as mandated by the Constitution, comprises the secretaries of the various departments of the Executive Office.

But these events still lay several hours in the future. For the moment, the SecDef was playing the role of warlord. As Saxon watched him on the screen, he had the impression, and not for the first time, that Hunnicut was mentally picturing himself as George C. Scott in the opening monologue of the movie *Patton.*

Hunnicut was a posturer—Saxon didn't like posturers. They were the kind who sat in the darkness of movie theaters on Sunday nights laughing at simulated death while the real thing was meted out to his soldiers in the field. Posturers returned to work the following morning, but when his men caught a bullet, the only place to which they returned was the cold embrace of mother earth.

Saxon's was not to reason why, though. He was an officer and a Marine, and part of what he was meant taking a lot of bullshit from brass hats, politicians, and their flacks, fags, and flunkies. As a soldier he was paid to fight, to kill, and to die, and principally in that order. Generals died in bed, or so at least went the saying. It could be added that politicians usually went out that way, too.

For all of that it was a field command that any soldier worth his rifle wanted more than anything else. Saxon was thankful that he wasn't baby-sitting and diapering a desk at the Pentagon right now. To Saxon's thinking this was truly a fate worse than even death. Only the intervention of General "Patient K" Kullimore—whose soldiering skills were equaled, and at times exceeded, by his Puzzle Palace veteran's skills at working the Byzantine Defense Department system—had saved Saxon from that gruesome fate.

Patient K had more channels connecting into Foggy Bottom power centers than a cable TV. Though it was the general who had ordered Saxon to the White House in the aftermath of the oil riots that had marked the close of the global spasm of violence caused by the Mahdi's attacks on petroleum centers, calling Saxon away from action in Yemen and Oman, the president had expressly asked for the meeting.

An old Building hand, Kullimore also knew that nothing in Washington ever took place in a complete vacuum, and that the enemies of Marine Force One at the Defense Department had been given a ready-made opportunity to corral Saxon into a staff position stateside and pave the way to ease him from command of the Big Mean One. After that, Saxon could be replaced with a CO whose job at MF-1 was actually the dismantling, and not the leadership, of the elite Marine brigade.

Marine Force One had been Kullimore's vision—a self-contained go-anywhere, do-anything strike force of super infantry, able to field any mission at any place on the globe before any other outfit could get there.

Marine Force One was an army within an army, a power within a power. Its reach was global, its commitment to the mission total. It flew, it swam, it walked, it rolled. It became whatever it needed to become in order to do the job.

The force could turn on a dime, take itself apart, and put itself back together to field multiple missions in regional theaters around the world. MF-1's reliance on a network-centric approach to warfare insured that those scattered forces were connected to each other, to One's Pentagon-based command center, and to joint commands on sea, land, air, and space.

If the USMC was the spear-point of U.S. military forces, then the Big Mean One was the razor-sharp tip of that cutting edge. If the Marines were the eagle, then MF-1 was the eagle's flexed talons. These analogies did not sit well with other specialist formations that each claimed to fill these operational roles.

The USN in particular did not appreciate what certain highly placed brass perceived as another analogy. They looked at Marine Force One as a modern Prometheus stealing fire from the gods, those divinities being the Navy's prized SEALs. But—

"Colonel Saxon?"

Saxon realized he'd let his mind wander.

The SecDef had directed a question to him, but Saxon's mind had been focused on other things. Not hard to go elsewhere when Hunnicut's verbal diarrhea filled the air, Saxon thought. Saxon had a low tolerance for crap of any kind and tried to keep upwind of it. Hunnicut's sanctimonious and long-winded speech had opened the toilet door.

"Sir?"

"Colonel Saxon," Hunnicut was saying, his voice now having grown petulant, "the president wants to feel especially confident about the prospect of capturing Evangelista. As you know, Evangelista, 'the Evangelist,' as his supporters know him, is viewed by this administration as the last terrorist chieftain of any note on our list, the final link in the chain connecting Saddam Hussein, bin Laden, the Mahdi, and Stavar Zahlenko."

Hunnicut let the question hang in the air. Saxon wanted to tell this fucker that he didn't have a crystal ball. He couldn't predict when they'd capture Evangelista or bring his head back on a platter.

"We're doing our best, Mr. Secretary," he answered.

"The president—"

"Warren," one of the backseaters chimed in on the conference link, "everything's in place. We can't predict the outcome of the operations. We're soldiers, not soothsayers. I've informed the president that he can be optimistic, that's the best anyone can do under the circumstances."

The defense secretary nodded. In his office everything was neat as a pin as he gestured to a Marine orderly wheeling a tray laden with coffee and danishes toward him. Out of camera range, the SecDef gestured with his index finger at one sugar-glazed delicacy and then another, which the orderly gingerly placed on a warm plate with silver tea service tongs and set the plate gently atop the secretary's desk. He then set a carafe of piping hot black coffee next to the pastries and decorously took his leave.

Hunnicut would have a little nosh before departing his office, although there would probably be some of those nice deli sandwiches at the White House. Hunnicut was a strategist. A graduate of Yale, where he'd been a Skull and Bones man, and later on, a Smithsonian fellow. Hunnicut had never shed a drop of blood in combat. To such as him the world outside was a projection of the orderly and symmetrical vision inside the heads of policymakers, not the messy and often insane Shakesperean tragedy it more often turned into.

In short, Hunnicut and his expectations were totally off the wall. But then again, so were the goals and expectations of the self-styled revolutionaries and self-appointed freedom fighters whose grandiose delusions had been translated into nightmare scenarios for the last thirty years in a cycle of terrorist attacks and counterterrorist warfare. Men like Saxon were caught in between the rocks and hard places of a world gone crazy and getting crazier by the minute.

Men like Saxon were the only sane ones. They were the only ones who knew the ground truth. They were the only ones who still gave a damn and were prepared to do something about it. Saxon told the SecDef that he was good to go. The SecDef replied that this was good enough for him, but the smile he flashed was a purely fuck-you tightening of the lips, a spasmodic twitch that was as much grimace as smile—Hunnicut probably looked that way when taking medicine, screwing his wife, or using the john, Saxon reflected.

But he didn't care. Saxon was a warrior. He would do what he was paid to do—his job, and everything that was implied by the term. So would his men. They, like himself, were warriors. They, like himself, were US Marines.

And they were doing that job right now, out in the jungles of Amazonia, far off in the arid mountain country of the Caucasus, in the arid deserts of North Africa, and on the heaving waters of the South China Sea approaching the Sunda Straits.

The go-anywhere, do-anything brigade that was Marine Force One was there at the epicenters of the world's strategic hot spots. Soldiering on. Fighting, bleeding, dying. Doing the jobs that no other force would or could do, nor which the politicians who sent them there to do them even vaguely understood.

Prop noise filled the air as the CH-130H lumbered on through still-dark skies over dense subtropical jungle. The Hercules had descended to just below treetop height. On the flight deck and in the aft cargo compartment, all aircrew were aware that the plane was now picking up small-arms fire.

Bullets spanged the wings. That's what the partisans concealed down there beneath the foliage often shot for—the wings, not the fuselage.

The Evangelist's *guerilleros* were trained to shoot for the wings. Their goal was to bring the plane down and not totally destroy the *yanqui* aircraft.

A downed cargo plane was usually a source of many useful goodies, courtesy of Uncle Sam. A crashed cargo plane, on the other hand, was just a bunch of smoldering, burning junk. So they shot for the wings most of the time. They were doing this right now as the prop-driven plane steadily spilled altitude.

Inside the plane, the loadmaster had just received the command to drop the cargo. It was a big sucker. A fifteen-ton Block Two Massive Ordnance Air Blast Bomb or MOAB-II, a descendent of the BLU-82 Daisy Cutter that first debuted in 'Nam. Those shits down in the jungle were about to get more than they bargained for, the loadmaster knew.

He pushed the buttons that opened the hydraulically actuated rear cargo hatch. Let them chew on this baby, he thought with a smile as he signaled his crew to shove the pallet toward the patch of deep blue sky showing out the rear of the plane.

Way to go, bitch he thought, *way to fuckin' go.*

chapter *five*

The island of Aruba sits between seventy and eighty degrees latitude at the top of the continental landmass of South America, midway between the isthmus of Panama and the far smaller island archipelagos of St. Vincent and the Grenadines. Out beyond the island chains lies the vast southern expanse of the Atlantic Ocean, some three thousand miles of open sea at whose other shores lie the continents of Europe and Africa.

Equipped with a compass and a map, a seafarer can easily chart a course from Aruba to any number of exciting and entertaining ports of call in Europe, Africa, and the nations that border the shores of the Mediterranean Sea, which can be reached through the Straits of Gibraltar at the other end of the Atlantic. Such a journey is both scenic and adventurous, and—with modern vessels equipped with the latest in high-technology gear able to detect oncoming squalls and icebergs—is also completely safe.

For this reason, and because Aruba itself is a tourist mecca, the Atlantic crossing between the island nation and distant ports half a world away make Aruba an excellent place for cruise lines to do business. Aruba's ports bustle with shipping of every kind, but passenger liners make up the greater percentage of Aruba's shipping traffic on a day-to-day basis.

The influx of tourists to this vacation and travel mecca have made Aruba a world-class resort area rivaling the chic rivieras of Italy and the south of France. High on the bluffs above the corniche that commands excellent views of the marinas where the yachts owned by the global super-rich are berthed nestle the whitewashed, pale pink and yellow villas of the well-to-do.

One such villa was the Villa Marengo, which occupied a four-acre plot in a prime real estate section of the city. The Villa Marengo was equipped with an indoor and outdoor pool and lush palm trees providing cool shade in the heat of the afternoon.

A staff of two servants and a live-in chef were permanently attached to the Villa Marengo, which was owned by one Mohammad Al Serif. Serif was a well-known international department store magnate whose holdings included the largest stores on London's Oxford Street, Paris's Champs Élysées, and New York's Fifth Avenue.

Al Serif, an Egyptian, saw fit to hire his own nationals in his far-flung business empire. Such was the chef, whose credentials included being the head *chef de cuisine* at one of Cairo's most fashionable eateries, and who spent the off-season cooking for rentiers of the Villa Marengo. The chef's name was Moofzi Al Ahard, and he was simultaneously a member of Egypt's Muslim Brotherhood; a man committed to the downfall of his employer and benefactor Al Serif. The department store magnate, shrewd businessman that he was, had never suspected a thing.

In addition to his culinary masterpieces, the chef at the Villa Marengo kept his eyes open for opportunities that played into the hands of the Brotherhood and the assorted terrorist cadres to which they were allied.

The present guests at the Villa Marengo loved

Al Ahard's exquisite French cooking. He wished he could have poisoned the bastards, once a quick check of the Internet confirmed his suspicions about who they actually were and what they represented in terms of the struggle to whose ultimate success the chef was committed.

Encrypted messages sent over the Internet would make sure that the intelligence the chef had gathered would reach the right people—people who could use the villa's current occupants as pawns in a larger, more terrible, and far bloodier game than the one they enjoyed playing in the afternoon heat.

The loadmaster aboard the Hercules gave the signal to the dropmasters to slide the load out the back, which was now open and showing aquamarine sky as the dawn approached. This they did.

The pallet slid to the edge and didn't even teeter. The forward momentum of the aircraft put approximately sixty feet of distance between it and the pallet within three seconds of its sailing off the plane and into thin air.

A moment later it began to fall, and as it did the cargo's main chute deployed. The skids beneath it fell away as the huge silk jellyfish bellied out in the hot exhaust of the C-130's prop wash.

Tied to cables that hung thirty feet down from the chute canopy, the MOAB swung back and forth in the wind as it sailed earthward. It didn't have a very long journey ahead of it.

The munition, which at a half-kiloton of explosive force, was the most powerful non-nuclear or conventional explosive in the arsenal of democracy—or anybody else's for that matter—would descend to its detonation altitude in under four minutes, give or take. At that point a barometrically actuated electronic detonator on a microchip set behind the bomb's nose cone would trigger the explosive chain. A great deal of destruction would follow.

The MOAB-II was a fuel-air explosive, or FAE, unlike previous MOAB types. The super-munition detonated to produce airbursts as opposed to groundbursts. You wanted a groundburst under certain conditions, such as when you wanted to pulverize an underground bunker that wasn't too deeply buried, or to be deployed in conjunction with a JDAM strike.

You wanted a nice-sized airburst under other circumstances—for example, if you needed to clear a patch of forested area by quickly and efficiently generating enough concussive force to knock down a couple of thousand trees that would otherwise be in the way of your troops while affording shelter to unfriendlies.

That's just what the MOAB was good at doing. The munition had been deployed to perform precisely this service in Afghanistan. It was about to do so once again, over a patch of jungle instead of arid mountains, in a different war under a different set of geostrategic circumstances.

None of this mattered to the bomb. The bomb had no politics and no conscience. The bomb could only explode.

As the seconds ticked down to the zero mark, the bomb continued its unhindered descent. In those final seconds before detonation, the crew on the flight deck of the Hercules were pouring every once of torque that the plane's four turboprop power plants were able to deliver toward arcing the plane around and getting it as far away from ground zero as quickly as possible.

The bomb continued to drop to its preset detonation altitude.

In the instant before detonation, the second-growth jungle below was still undisturbed.

A moment passed, and then another.

And another, and another.

The barometric pressure sensor inside the munition's nose assembly that was linked to a GPS receiver onboard the Hercules actuated the detonation sequence.

Another moment passed.

Suddenly a ring of nozzles simultaneously sprayed a cloud of fine and highly flammable mist into the air. This cloud of micro-fine droplets quickly spread out into a circle some thirty feet in diameter.

Observers on the ground could actually see the deadly cloud sparkle as it caught and refracted the rays of the subequatorial sun. The rainbow effect was strikingly beautiful to behold, like the harbinger of some heavenly boon that was about to descend on the jungle below.

Anything but a boon. More like a boom. A very big, very loud, very bad boom.

In the fevered beat of a racing pulse, the initiator charge exploded, igniting the droplet cloud of gasoline-derivative. The cloud caught fire in under a millisecond. The rapid-ignition chain reaction generated a blast wave with the equivalent force of tons of pressure against the jungle below.

Trunks of trees snapped clear of their roots amid a vortex of flame and concussion. The rapid conflagration also consumed all the oxygen in the surrounding atmosphere, creating an instantaneous vacuum. Into this vacuum rushed enveloping air with such speed that a thunderclap was generated that boomed and rolled for miles as it bounced from peak to peak of the surrounding mountainsides.

In the aftermath of the concussive airburst, a roughly circular area had been cleared sufficient to permit the unobstructed landing of rotary wing aircraft while affording a free field of fire to combat jets and helo gunships that would cover the landing of troops.

As the blast died away there came the faint but steadily building drone and clamor of the Ospreys. Operation Big Thunder had begun in earnest. It had started off auspiciously—with a bang.

The Mexican maid had been brought up in a small village not far from Cancun under a strict moral and religious code. She was still devout. She did not like many of the carryings-on of the American and European tourists for whom she kept house.

Aruba's beaches were topless, and the clientele of many of the villas also enjoyed casual nudity. These present guests were no exception. Unfortunately, the maid had nowhere else to go. She had to put up with it or find work elsewhere. And there was no other work to be found.

The couple who had rented the place was now sitting at the swimming pool's bar. The bar was inset into the side of the pool and there were seats built into the bottom of the pool, at the shallow end, where swimmers could pause from their frolicking in the water and sip cold, refreshing drinks. The maid was acting as bartender.

The *yanqui* woman sat bare-breasted. Her long dark nipples were erect. The man was completely nude. You could see something resembling a snake or a large worm through the shallow water, and the gringo made no attempt to hide this thing of his. He also saw no shame in fondling the woman's breasts in full view of the maid as both sipped their piña coladas.

From time to time he looked at the maid in a way that was openly seductive. He did not say, "Come and join us, *mamasita,*" but it was understood from his glance that this was what he was thinking. The maid pretended not to notice. These two *yanquis* were both drunk by now on their stinking piña coladas. Their shame was their own. She, who was forced to suffer their presence, was blameless, of this the maid was sure.

Soon the two *yanquis* pushed off into the center of the swimming pool. The maid did not linger.

She did not want to see what they were doing there, in the water. The sounds they were making were bad enough and told her the entire tale as she hurried from the poolside.

The Evangelist only too well understood that his number was up in the instant he heard the blast and saw what looked like a nuclear mushroom cloud rise up on a pedestal of churned-up earth to spread its roiling brown toadstool of smoke over the jungle canopy.

His men fell on their faces. They cried out in terror that the gringos had unleashed an atomic weapon upon them. Evangelista tried to calm them down.

He told them that this was not that sort of weapon.

"See the shape of this cloud? See the manner in which this cloud spreads? It would be considerably different were it a nuke that had been detonated by the gringos. No, *mis compañeros,* the gringos had merely used one of their largest conventional bombs, this and nothing more.

"And to what purpose was this bomb used? Compadres, it was a bomb of a type that these *yanqui pendejos* had developed to clear landing zones. To clear them quickly, so that many men could be deployed in a short period of time. Of a type to clear landing zones, but not of the nuclear variety of bomb, no.

"This," he told his men, "may spell as much

trouble for you, if not more, than a nuclear blast, *compadres*. I will not lie to you, my brave comrades. For it means that the gringo *cabrones* have begun their long-awaited spring offensive. We have prepared for this, yes, but now that it is upon us we must be far braver than we have ever been before.

"The *yanquis* will use every weapon at their disposal. They have been trained to attack with great speed and ferocity. They will attack our guerilla fighters from the air and on the ground alike. They will send in men to assault us at close range and they will send in their damned cruise missiles from far away. You have seen all of this many times before. You all know what the Americans are capable of doing. But remain steadfast and do what your commanders have trained you to do, and you will prevail against these *yanqui* dogs."

Evangelista spat on the ground.

"Do you know what I say to these *pendejos, amigos?* I say, *Me cago en sus madres!*"

The men cheered this boldness. Their leader could see a new light come into their eyes. He had reached them, as he had always been able to do.

El Magnifico was an inspiring sight, and his men believed him. But the guerilla chieftain himself held no comforting illusions concerning the likelihood of success.

The Americans were about to roll all over everything. He had seen it coming for months, and through the winter rainy season had prepared his ratline. There was no alternative to the ratline.

Escape was an imperative when facing imminent defeat—escape, or death, and Evangelista had not yet reached the point where he felt compelled to fall on his sword in the manner of old Roman generals.

On the contrary, that way out was the foot soldiers' lot in his vision of warfare. War was a business to him. As much as it was to the international defense contractors who built the gunships and the guidance systems for the Tomahawk missiles that were already being programmed with the coordinates of his encampments in the jungle.

In his role as the leader, Evangelista's presence was necessary to keep the arms industry that was getting rich from this war in clover. To keep them producing. To keep the money rolling in. If the Evangelist did not exist, the arms merchants would have needed to have invented him. In a way, that's just what had taken place.

Evangelista knew that his enemies could have crushed him years before. But it was more profitable to let him go on a bit longer. Yet it had just become apparent that his survival was no longer deemed a necessary evil.

And so now he was about to cash in his chips and leave the game. There were other options for him, if not for his loyal troops. Evangelista estimated that the encampment in which he now stood with his men would be reduced to wreckage in only a few more hours.

It was time to move. He had an appointment with destiny—and the first stop on his prearranged escape route.

The vessel dwarfed everything else in the harbor. She was a manmade leviathan, a prodigy of the seas. Her builders had intended her to be that and more besides. The *King Albert III* was conceived and built to be the world's largest and most lavishly appointed cruise liner. The ship was a self-contained floating city.

Her tiers of decks rose more than seven stories above the water, making the liner not only taller than the tallest of the buildings in Aruba, but taller than those in many a small city anywhere on earth. All together, those stacks of decks comprised as much surface area as a small town. Moreover, the *King Albert III* was equipped with more amenities than any small town could offer.

The cruise liner boasted seven shops selling

every variety of goods from consumer electronics to designer condoms. The ship maintained its own fully staffed hospital and boasted the only floating MRI diagnostic machinery outside of hospital ships, and her fully trained medical staff, including a skilled neurosurgeon, meant she could rival even these. Her ballrooms would play host to international talent that not even the most renowned casinos on the Vegas strip could attract. Her companionways and staterooms were designed by Europe's most skilled architects and hung with artwork from trendy Soho galleries.

The liner had docked in Aruba the previous day for refueling, refitting, and revictualizing. The *King Albert III* would also take on a large number of passengers. Travel agencies used Aruba as a pass-through access point for international cruiseline bookings.

Almost a third of the *King Albert*'s passengers had debarked permanently on the island tourist spot. Their berths would be filled by passengers who were boarding from Aruba to travel to cross-Atlantic destinations in North Africa, Europe, and the Mediterranean.

Among those embarking passengers were the couple who had spent their last week sunning themselves at Villa Marengo. They had booked a lavish stateroom with an in-suite bathroom on the topmost tier of the ship.

Their ultimate destination was the city of Marrakech, Morocco. There they were expected at the sumptuous villa of an American newspaper magnate who had made certain that the couple would have everything at their disposal necessary to insure their month-long stay at the estate would be a happy and memorable one.

En route to Marrakech the ship was scheduled to dock at several ports of call, including the rock of Gibraltar, the Balearic Islands, and Agadir, a city located close to Marrakech. The couple planned to visit these places, too—extending their stay should they find them appealing—before moving on to Marrakech.

The passage across the Atlantic would take ten days, according to the ship's schedule. It could have been accomplished in far less time, but this wasn't the U.S. Sixth Fleet; it was a pleasure cruise, and the ship would take its time.

Guests would enjoy the finest food and entertainment on any ship to ever make the crossing, amid the most exquisite surroundings possible throughout the voyage. The American couple that had embarked at Aruba was looking forward to making the trip, as all of the other new passengers were. They all had heard that the cruise was considered by many to be the experience of a lifetime.

They were not about to be disappointed. Their voyage was destined to be an experience that few had ever had before. Only it wasn't to be quite the same as anybody had planned, or even envisioned.

chapter *six*

"Lord, how I love the Marines!"

Sergeant Death was puking his guts out. Something to do with the water. Or the paramecia inside the water. Or maybe it was the bumpy ride on the Osprey.

Detachment Gamma was one of One's modular forces. Gamma had been assigned to Sector Ollie, a region of dense jungle interspersed with some of the many tributaries of the Amazon River. Sergeant Death was Gamma's top kick.

"Every day's a payday in the Marines!" Sergeant Death went on tossing his cookies. "Every night's a party. Every minute in the Marines is better than the one that came before."

The NCO leaned over the side of the patrol boat and vomited again. After that he felt much better. The thunderstorm in his guts was passing, he thought. He'd remember to stick with bottled beer from now on. Fuck the water. A Marine shouldn't drink that shit anyway. From now on, beer or nothing. It would be his soldier's creed.

The riverine patrol boat chugged down the muddy river. Behind it were two more of the same type. Marines crouching behind deck guns cast wary gazes at the deceptively deserted riverbanks. They knew that any number of unpleasant things could be concealed behind the tree line.

For the moment the patrol was on its own, but backup was expected. Attack helos were in transit with an ETA of fifteen minutes. The patrol's destination was a suspected *guerillero* stronghold deep in a remote jungle area identified on tactical maps as Sector Alpha. The camp was protected by natural foliage barriers through which armor couldn't effectively maneuver, and where any force above squad level would instantly be sighted by enemy patrols long before it could reach the target.

Since defoliants had been banned, and the use of MOABs and similar munitions limited to high-value targets only, this meant that riverine troops and close air support (CAS) was the force mixture of choice. Operationally, this arrangement was a throwback to the Korean and Vietnam wars.

During the Cold War, and for decades afterward, airborne assets supported armor, not infantry.

Network-centric warfare made CAS again viable for ground warfare operations. Troops digitally tied into a sensor grid that was shared with strike and surveillance aircraft could function as a unified organism.

Out to three hundred miles or more, AWACS aircraft orbited the operational sectors of Amazonia. AWACS could not only keep tabs on any hostile aircraft or missiles, but its ground radar also could keep watch on the terrain below. More sophisticated than AWACS for ground reconnaissance and surveillance were J-STARS planes, which used an array of more powerful look-down radars in conjunction with ground station modules (GSMs).

Both these aircraft were linked to friendly air such as Comanche helos, F-22 Raptors, or F-35 Joint Strike Fighters. The fighter planes were based forward of the operational sectors, pre-positioned at FOLs so they could reach troops in the jungle within minutes and bring down a deadly array of fires on unfriendlies. They were also based on carriers anchored offshore, where they were maintained in a state of constant readiness.

The legs knew where the air was at all times and vice versa. Strikes could be called in with high speed and great accuracy. Communications gear was lightweight and integrated into each foot soldier's equipment.

The enemy was not as well equipped as U.S. forces, but unfriendlies had all the time-tested advantages of operating on familiar terrain working in their favor. They were adept at setting up mantraps and booby traps of every conceivable variety.

Evangelista's insurgency forces had been playing merry hell with Colombian, Ecuadorian, and Brazilian forces for the last decade using such guerilla tactics. They had beaten back national troops and made incursions into the major cities of the three countries in which they operated. They held most of the outlying districts, too.

It was when the Evangelist exported the revolution to the United States that the president increased U.S. Operation Colombia forces into an expeditionary force dedicated to rooting out the partisan insurgents.

The attacks on guerilla bases had begun the previous fall. With the coming of the rainy season in the winter, the military actions had abated. Now, with the monsoon rains ended, a long-planned major push to oust the insurgents from their jungle strongholds had begun in earnest.

The Marines were part of it.

Marine Force One led the way.

Sergeant Death knew about the larger objectives of the campaign and its importance to the fight against global terrorism. So did his men. At the moment, though, this political and historical framework wasn't in the forefront of his thoughts. At the moment, Death was chugging upriver on a patrol boat with his rifle trained on the river's left bank. Specialist One-Eyes was in position behind the minigun mounted atop the boat's central gun turret, his attention moving from bank to bank as he scanned the perimeter for signs of trouble.

The electrically driven automatic weapon was beltfed and capable of spitting out an amazing number of 7.62mm bullets in an amazingly short span of time. The belt was loaded with a three-to-one ratio of green tracers to standard ammo.

In a firefight, the tracers would help Private One-Eyes walk his fire where it did the enemy the most harm. Tracer fire would also allow him to paint the target for shooters aboard the patrol boat and for

WSOs in friendly air called in to provide riverine forces with close support.

Sergeant Death was still singing the praises of the Corps, but now sotto voce, as his steely gray eyes scanned the banks of the river. The sergeant's combat reflexes urged silence and vigilance. The sun was partly obscured by low-hanging cloud cover. A milky gray-white light played across the landscape, which was a study in browns and greens.

The riverbanks were fringed with dark green, burnt-looking scrub growth, cactus and agaves, and the bizarrely twisted trunks of densely packed mangroves, but true, double-canopy jungle began only a few hundred meters or so beyond the edge of the water.

From the darkness beyond the fringe of vegetation there came the strident calls of birds and the occasional rustling of leaves as something or other moved rapidly across the tops of the verdant canopy. The silence was eerie and ominous, and it quickly told on the nerves.

At the first sign of surprise movement, fingers tightened on triggers and pulses quickened with the expectation of contact with the enemy. This was bandit country. All of the members of the patrol knew of the danger of ambush by partisan forces. Sector Ollie belonged to Evangelista rebel troops.

As the Marines of Detachment Gamma moved toward their objective, they felt the presence of hostile eyes on them.

It was easy for the mind to conjure up a jungle teeming with enemy troops, all of them pointing their weapons at the riverine patrol. It was easy to view yourself as a sitting duck. You felt exposed. Alone. You almost wished something would happen, because you felt that a firefight was inevitable, and you might as well get it over with sooner rather than later.

Anything was better than the tension that mounted and built until it reached the point where it was almost unendurable.

But nothing happened. No attack came. The patrol boats moved slowly up the lazy, turbid waters of the muddy Rio Negro. They would reach their RV point with the arriving gunships in approximately one hour more.

"Man, I love the Marines," Sgt. Death repeated softly, wiping the sweat from his eyes as his finger gripped the trigger of his combat rifle. "Every day's a—"

He stopped just in time to get to the side of the boat and puke some more.

In Sector Charlie all hell was now breaking loose. In this northwestern region of Amazonia, a huge expanse of jungle had been leveled by the single MOAB that had been dropped to prep the area for attack by friendly troops.

Tall jungle trees had been felled like matchsticks. The stench of high explosive and massive burning filled the air. A haze of gray-blue smoke from scattered blazes drifted over a wide swath of territory. The smell of gasoline was somewhere in there, mixed up with other odors that had become part and parcel of modern war.

The sector was alive with the sounds of aircraft of many types. The first to enter the battle zone were Osprey convertiplanes. These shuttled troops and their weapons and gear—including fast-attack vehicles of various kinds—into the sector.

Marine AH-1W Whiskey Cobra attack helos escorted the Ospreys at low altitude where they were exposed to SAM fire from the jungle. The SAMs came in a full variety of flavors, ranging from small, shoulder-fire launchers of the SA-7, Stinger, or Blowpipe types, to mobile SA-10 and SA-11 surface-to-air missile launchers that were capable of tracking and engaging the high-flying fast-movers of the U.S. air force.

There was still a lot of enemy down in there. The

MOAB had cleared away a square half-mile of jungle, but beyond the circle of scorched earth the guerillas were still in business. They would not go down easy.

The Evangelist's forces also had mobile antiaircraft artillery and fixed emplacements that were cunningly concealed amid the shadowed depths of the jungle. They presented anything but a paper target. As the Ospreys came in to ferry ground troops into the combat sector, the *guerilleros* were launching missile salvos at them and unleashing fusillades of savage small-arms fire with the ferocity and tenacity of the doomed.

Mortars, the bane of infantry, had also opened up on the forces now landing in theater. In well-concealed emplacements in the hillsides surrounding the cleared terrain, mortar crews equipped with eight-inch tubes were shooting HESH rounds into the air. They were expertly walking their fire in on the Ospreys and the combatants running from the LZs into attack-defense positions near the perimeter.

El Evangelista's men didn't have satellite coverage, but they had well-trained and keen-eyed spotters concealed amid the dense growth of forested ridge lines overlooking the helo landing zones.

Equipped with grid maps, high-power binoculars, and secure encrypted radios, the spotters were reporting the exact fire positions to the mortar crews, and doing so with a high level of accuracy. As a result, the arriving troops hit the ground running amid the boiling chaos of a hot LZ that was going on all around them.

Men fell as high explosive and splinter clouds of hot shrapnel cooked off bursting shells and ripped into their bodies. The mortar fire was deadly and accurate. Evangelista's mortar crews were obviously crackerjack. They had set every third round to detonate as an airburst and their barrages to explode at different altitudes. The result was a hemisphere of time-on-target fire that was devastating to the arriving Marines and took a considerable toll on men and combat machinery.

Several million dollars worth of Osprey was destroyed in this manner by a salvo of mortar rounds costing only a few hundred pesos. The number-two transport ship had just unloaded its last soldier, and the troops were away into the bush.

The Osprey, now in helo mode with its rotor nacelles tilted upward, was lifting off the LZ as a serics of mortar airbursts detonated within a few meters of the ascending aircraft. Fragments of whirling, white-hot shrapnel sliced through the fuselage and penetrated the crew compartment and fuel bladders. Although the fuel mixture was not highly flammable, the explosive force and incandescent metal splinters were sufficient to cause the system to overheat.

More to the point, the burst also crippled the pilot, whose loss of control caused the Osprey to pitch violently to one side. The whirling rotor blades of the convertiplane sent it careening through the air at a crazy angle until it slammed into the side of a hill. A fireball wreathed in oily black smoke erupted from the vegetation, and a trail of twisted wreckage was strewn all over the LZ and surrounding terrain.

The other three Ospreys engaged in troop landing operations were spared destruction as they lifted off and made quick transits from the landing zones. They had debarked their men and cargos and were now heading back to base. Some of the aircraft had sustained damage from minor hits, but were intact enough to return under their own steam.

The Marines in the landing force had fanned out into the jungle where they were immediately met with heavy enemy resistance. The interior of the jungle underbrush seemed to have come alive with tracer fire and multiple explosions. The Marines returned fire, aiming at the muzzle flashes of the *guerilleros* concealed in the underbrush. Rockets crisscrossed through the dark interior of the jungle, and shell bursts rocked and tore at the earth. When the munitions' thunder finally died away, the sound of wounded men hollering for medics filled the humid air.

The first wave of Marines faced an enemy bent on throwing them back in any way possible. From out of the jungle the defending forces hurled themselves at the invaders in a frontal attack.

The Marines of Force One were equipped with AKS-74 Krinov automatic rifles. These Kalashnikovs had been found to be far more reliable and more deadly than general-issue M-4s or M-16s. The Kaloshes also were better fitted to the use of bayonets in close-in fighting. Colonel David Saxon had made certain that bayonet fighting was taught and practiced by all Marine Force One members. The deadly skill had come in handy on previous missions.

Now, as the contending forces closed and clashed, Marines and *guerilleros* became embroiled in vicious close-quarter fighting. Men were shot at close range, or stabbed in the belly by bayonets and combat knives, or simply pummeled by a pair of fists when no other weapon was available.

The dull reports of grenade explosions and the rat-a-tat of small arms fire, the banshee wail and ripping-silk sound of incoming light artillery and mortar fire, the screams, shouts, and groans of men fighting for their lives or giving up their ghosts in the thick of battle, filled the air as the Marines were locked in combat with Evangelista's partisans for control of a foot of earth in the darkness of the primeval jungle.

In Sector Alpha, Sergeant Death's lips stopped in the middle of his familiar mantra.

"I love the Ma—"

What was it?

A glint of light on metal, or was he imagining things? The riverine patrol was now getting close to its target. Did the sergeant imagine hearing the faint rustle of movement that seemed manmade as opposed to the natural sounds of the jungle?

Death glanced toward Specialist One-Eyes. The trooper nodded behind the minigun. He'd sensed or seen something, too. The rest of the crew had also noticed it. Death radioed the other two patrol boats to remain alert.

And then, with a suddenness that made the heart stop and a thrill of adrenaline shoot along the nerves, all hell was breaking loose.

Tracers streamed in from the banks, leaving incandescent tracks in the air. The fire was concentrated on the riverine patrols. Rocket strikes followed, blowing holes in the water surrounding the boats and sending up huge gouts of white, frothing wetness. The rapid chatter of the lead craft's minigun answered the fire from the banks as Specialist One-Eyes opened up. From behind the first boat, automatic defensive fire started up as the MGs and small arms onboard came alive and did their lethal work. Marines shouted and cursed and kept their fingers curled on the triggers of their chattering weapons.

From the accuracy and concentration of the incoming, Sgt. Death was convinced that the convoy of patrol boats had probably been watched for some time. The *guerilleros* had been biding their time. Stealthily, slowly, they had moved men and guns to positions on the bank near target vector H-1, which they knew as El Camino Rojo, the Red Road. For all the technological superiority of the gringos, the partisan's creed was that mastery of the ancient arts of jungle warfare could still overcome any enemy.

As fire chattered all around them, Sgt. Death was on SINCGARS radio, calling in friendly air.

"Thunder Three to Eagle Talon," the AWACS controller who was sitting in an air-conditioned compartment hundreds of miles to the southeast and twenty-five thousand feet in the air said back to the Marine who was already drenched with foul-smelling, muddy river water. "Top cover's on the way. ETA five minutes."

Two fast-movers—Marine F-35 Joint Strike Fighters—had been flying combat air patrol within a few miles of the riverine patrol's position. They had been dispatched by AWACS to get them out of trouble.

"I copy," Sgt. Death responded to AWACS.

He passed the word to the rest of the men over the comms net. They were to hold fast until CAS arrived.

This was easier said than done, though. Five minutes might get you ten anywhere else, but in combat even a minute could fast become a lifetime. Enemy fire from both banks of the river was increasing in tempo and intensity as the moments passed. The crews aboard the patrol boats were beginning to run out of ammo as the clock ticked down to zero.

Suddenly, in the midst of the din of battle, there was the scream of firewalled ramjet engines as USAF Raptors out of the nearest FOL screamed down on the fire zone in supercruise mode. They wasted no time in putting the enemy through hell. AIM-10 Super Sparrow missiles, upgraded and optimized for low-intensity warfare environments, screamed down from the F-22s' internal weapons dispensers. The missiles struck their earthbound targets with pinpoint accuracy. A ripple of multiple explosions drowned out the deadly chatter of enemy small arms. After the explosions, the sound of gunfire suddenly cut off, as if a switch had been thrown.

Their morale boosted, the survivors of the ambush on the river opened up from their patrol boats, spraying the jungle with MG fire. The F-22s meanwhile heeled around and slammed more deadly munitions strikes into the unfriendlies hunkered in the jungle. It was all over as quickly and as suddenly as it had started. The Raptors wiggled their wings in salute to the Marines and flew off.

"Man, I love the Marines," Sgt. Death groaned through clenched teeth as a medic tended to the ragged shrapnel wound on his left arm.

The odd thing about it, thought the medic, as he dressed the wound and applied a pressure bandage, was that the sergeant probably wasn't even joking.

chapter *seven*

Now on the run, the guerilla chieftain was at leisure to reflect on his life as he made a break for freedom. Carlos Evangelista's career as a partisan fighter had begun during the event that had come to be known as "Colombia's 9/11," and whose violence had nearly equalled the attacks on America.

More than a decade before, radical M-19 guerilla squads had staged a massive raid on the government's Chamber of Deputies. The building was taken over and the deputies of the Colombian parliament held hostage for three tense days. The Colombian army would not negotiate. It adopted a scorched-earth policy: Troops opened fire on captives and captors alike. There were few survivors. The original building, too severely damaged by fires and explosions to be allowed to remain standing, was razed to the ground and a new one erected in its place.

Conspiracy charges continued to fly for years following the botched takeover, armed siege, and violent resolution of the incident. Evangelista had begun as special investigator to President Alfonzo Rodriguez. His investigation uncovered evidence of a conspiracy to tighten the grip on the reins of power by the hardliners in the Colombian government. Evangelista, a young state attorney at the time, became a target of death squads himself. To save his own life, he fled into the jungle.

There, in hiding with a few other idealistic companions, he was hunted by nationalist forces. Yet the mountains gave him protection, and his own partisans grew in number and strength as they befriended the villagers who lived on the land. In time, Evangelista began being called "El Emme," after "El Trabjador del Milagros," the Miracle Worker, after not only defeating a large force of national troops, but for having converted them to his cause following their surrender. Now El Emme was a hero to many in the country and many others abroad. Not since Fidel Castro had a guerilla chieftain so captured the imagination of the world.

But there was a darker, more sinister side to the partisan commander. Evangelista had either privately been this way all along or had become corrupted or insane while hunted by nationalist forces in the jungle. El Magnifico soon began to preach a political philosophy with a strange, twisted logic. He openly espoused the cause of Hassan Ramad Ali, the fanatical terrorist leader of Al Qadr, the Glory, who was known as the Mahdi. Eventually, the Evangelist's forces had allied themselves with the Mahdi's terrorist nexus, conducting attacks on American and European targets.

After the Mahdi's disappearance and possible death following the global catastrophe known as Strike Day, Evangelista allied himself with the Libyan dictator Benzi Al-Sharq, the Father Colonel, who had come to power after his predecessor Moammar Qaddafi's strange demise.

Al-Sharq, known to the West mostly as "The Shark" or "Sharky," had been one of Qaddafi's right-hand lackeys. One day Qaddafi disappeared after making a videotape in which he spoke of joining the hidden Imam and reappearing with him. It was mystical nonsense but well in keeping with many of Qaddafi's quasi-mystical pronouncements, of which he had made many in his later years.

In the same videotape, Qaddafi appointed as leader of Libya the man who later took the honorific title of Father Colonel. It was a position nobody questioned, because the Shark unleashed a wave of purges that insured that those who might question the legitimacy of his rule were no longer numbered among the living. Al-Sharq had immediately begun doing all the characteristically hostile things that Qaddafi had done, such as aligning himself with the neo-Soviets in an effort to become a regional superpower.

The new Soviet-Libyan axis was based on an exchange of petrodollars from Libya's extensive oil reserves for the latest weapon in the Soviet arsenal. During the so-called years of perestroika between the Soviets and the West, the Russians had actually been engaged in a covert arms race based on high-technology and stealth.

Throughout the early years of the 21st century the Russians were quietly arming much of the Third World and nonaligned nations with inexpensive arms and armament designed to rival and counter the more sophisticated—and costly—arms of the West.

Among these weapon systems were the same Sovremmeny-class frigates that the Soviets had supplied China. The Sovremmenys were stealthy and boasted sophisticated and powerful radars rivaling those of US Ticonderoga-class Aegis cruisers.

Also supplied to Libya by the Kremlin were the latest Project 877–class submarines that the West knew by the NATO designation "Kilo." The Kilos supplied to the Shark were also ultra-quiet diesel electric boats, and they were more current than the ones Iran had received some years before.

Possibly Al-Sharq's most prized acquisition, however, and the crown jewel of his order of battle, was his wing of Sukhoi SU-47 Berkut fighter planes. The aircraft, whose Russian name meant "Golden Eagle," were stealth fighters that, while not as low-observable as the frontline U.S. stealth warplanes—the F-117A and the F-22 Raptor—were easily as stealthy as the F-35 Joint Strike Fighter.

Beyond this, the Sukhois were more maneuverable and were equipped with the unique power that all Russian fighters had—for example, the ability to perform high-angle-of-attack maneuvers, such as the "Cobra," that no Western aircraft could duplicate without the risk of stalling.

Just as Moammar El Qaddafi had given shelter to Carlos the Jackal when he was on the run, so Al-Sharq had offered asylum to his compatriot, the Colombian Evangelist.

It was Libya that was the end of the ratline for Evangelista. But at the moment, this destination was a long way away. It was a long distance geographically as well as in less tangible regards, such as its distance from Evangelista's current state of mind.

At the moment, El Emme was bumping along a jungle road that was more mud-slick than highway toward the first stop on his long journey: the island of Aruba.

It was still some six hundred miles as the buzzard flies from his present position in the depths of the jungles of Amazonia.

Evangelista knew he would make it safely to the asylum offered by his waiting host. But he had no intention of coming to his Libyan benefactor empty-handed.

It was no accident that Evangelista had chosen Aruba as his point of debarkation for Libya. The partisan chieftain did nothing merely by accident.

As El Emme was grinding along the mountain road, his host, Al-Sharq, was in the office of his sumptious palace in Tripoli. The Shark was resplendant in the regalia of his office. In full dress uniform, cap, and sunglasses, he stood at one of the windows in the presidential palace that overlooked the Gulf of Sirte, a body of water straddling the northwestern reaches of the Med.

The shark of Libya looked out through the windows, his eyes screened behind the lenses of his dark aviators. The brim of his military cap, whose round top might have been a halo around his head, cast a shadow over his face as he turned from the window.

He had not been able to see it, but he knew it was out there.

The U.S. Sixth Fleet had sent a carrier strike group into the Gulf of Sirte. Just as Mussolini had once declared the entire Mediterranean "Mare Nostrum"—Our Sea—so the Shark had declared the Gulf of Sirte Libya's domain, extending out to thirty miles from the shore, far beyond the internationally recognized three-mile limit.

By doing so he had thrown the gauntlet down in front of the U.S., whose shipping through the Med routinely passed well within the new Libyan security zone. Qaddafi had tried a similar gambit and had lost, but Libya's new leader would not fail. If the United States fell for his bait, Al-Sharq would de-claw the American eagle before the eyes of the world. The Shark had been secretly assured that he had the means to do this.

As he turned to the men who had assembled in

his office, his mind cast back to the recent secret meeting between himself and a high-ranking member of the Soviet Politburo. The Soviet had led a three-member delegation: he represented the Kremlin and was empowered to speak directly for Soviet Premier Timoshenko. The second member was Colonel General Vassily Romanov of the Russian air force. The third member of the panel was Genya Vasilovka, who represented the Sukhoi design bureau.

The Shark had met them at a remote desert retreat in the arid fastness of Al-Gaddar, a distant expanse of wadis and flat, sandy countryside in the interior of the Libyan desert, some five hundred miles from its coastal capital, Tripoli.

The Shark had seen the helicopters emblazoned with the red star of the Soviet military appear and land. The two helos had lifted off hours before in the darkness of early morning from a desolate base in South Ossetsia and had flown a surveillance-safe route to the rendezvous point.

The visitors had been shown all the amenities of Bedouin hospitality as they entered the leader's tent. A sheep was slaughtered before their eyes, and the carcass taken away to be roasted over a fragrant fire of sandalwood and glazed with the wild honey of desert bees. After they had feasted, they got down to business.

The Russians had promised the Libyan leader that he would receive their new Berkut advanced tactical fighter, or *mnogofunksionalny frontovoi istrebitel,* a Russian term using "frontal aviation" instead of the Western "tactical" to describe the aircraft's designation. The plane surpassed Western stealth fighters in many critical respects. The advanced fighter plane would be flown by Russian pilots. All Al-Sharq needed to do was provoke an international incident. The Russians would take care of the rest. The Libyan leader had told them he would think the proposal over, but that he could give them his guarded and provisional assent right then and there.

That same night the Libyan dictator had a dream. In the dream, the hated U.S. president was carried off in the grasp of an enormous black eagle whose red talons were the shape of the star emblems of the Soviet air force. In the morning, the Shark had no doubts that it was his destiny to humble the United States as no other warlord before him had ever succeeded in doing.

In the months that followed the Libyan-Soviet agreement, secret underground bases in the desert had been established to train flight crews and house the new planes. The Soviets had assured the Libyan leader that Western spy satellites wouldn't detect the extensive excavation and construction activity.

Moscow had sophisticated technology available that would defeat all attempts at detection. When everything was ready, it was only necessary to make the open declaration of Libya's sovereignty over the Gulf of Sirte and the threat to take military action against any and all powers who did not respect it. The rest would follow in due course.

The Libyan shark now turned from the window and smiled at the assemblage gathered in his spacious office. This was the critical moment. He would announce to his military and political leaders that Libya was about to become a force to be feared among the nations of the world.

The *King Albert III* continued to take on passengers in Aruba. The gargantuan ocean liner, whose hull had ridden well above the waterline for the last three days, was seen to visibly sink below the surface as thousands of tons of cargo, victuals, supplies, and human bodies were added to her enormous bulk. At the helm of the vessel, a technical team sent by the shipping company that operated the boat was engaged in making final calibrations to her advanced loran, sonar, and radar suites.

These personnel wore photo-ID security tags to identify them. Hundreds of people, from guests to service staff, came aboard and left the vessel on any given day she spent in port. Any one of these could have harbored secret malign intentions, so an elaborate security screen had been put in operation to protect the boat and her passengers from harm. Security personnel placed all passengers through a baggage scanner and used handheld chemical sniffers to detect the presence of explosive devices.

Every system had loopholes, though. No screen was perfect, no barrier unbreachable. A vessel on the seas presented a security nightmare. The ship's security loopholes had been identified and exploited by those who had other plans for the *King Albert III* than a pleasure cruise vacation.

Those plans would soon become operational.

In the darkened combat information center (CIC) of the USS *Dwight D. Eisenhower*, a nuclear carrier of the Nimitz-class, crewmembers at their stations scanned display terminals, spoke on phones and into the mikes of lightweight headsets, manipulated mice and keyboards, and awaited orders from their commanding officers.

The *Eisenhower* had sailed to within a mile of Al-Sharq's self-imposed Zone of Death. The carrier battlegroup of which the *Eisenhower* was the heart was now arrayed in a stationary formation facing the shores of Libya, which boasted the port and capital city of Tripoli.

The *Eisenhower*'s skipper, Commander Harrison Butcher, awaited orders from CINCMED. So far, they were in a holding pattern. At the moment, a crisis meeting was taking place at the highest levels of political and military strategy of the United States.

In the National Security Council crisis room beneath the White House, and at the Pentagon's National Military Command Center in the Building's sub-basement, the midnight oil was being burned as strategic options were being considered. In these councils of war, factions faced each other across a divide as great as that which separated the United States and the small North African nation.

Nothing took place in a vacuum, and in the realm of international events this dictum was especially pertinent. Although the neo-Sovs had taken steps to circumvent U.S. surveillance efforts in the Libyan desert, they had not been entirely successful. Intelligence had leaked out that the Libyans were in league with the Russians, and that the Kremlin had embarked on a new strategy of international brinkmanship to exploit the tensions along the political fault lines of the world.

These fault lines occupied different places at

different times in history. During the Cold War, such cultural and economic fissures ran through the growing power centers of developing nations in the Third World. The Soviets had used military surrogates in Nicaragua, in El Salvador, in the Philippines, in Cuba, in Angola, and elsewhere to test the resolve of the West.

In the 21st century, the fault lines had shifted. They no longer extended through nation states as they had once done. The fissures now ran through what the Colombian terror chieftain, the Evangelist, had termed "the Archipelago."

By this, the partisan leader had meant something never seen before in the world—shadow states within nation states made up of both organized criminal enterprises in failed nations and guerilla insurgents in the jungles and deserts of the world.

The islands in this Archipelago stretched around the world, forming an invisible empire along the fault lines of modern civilization. If left to grow and metastasize, these centers of chaos and decay could envelop the healthy tissue of all nation states and destroy them like a fast-spreading cancer.

It was in the Archipelago that the neo-Sovs sought to refight the surrogate wars of the previous century, in much the same manner that the Cold War of the twentieth century was a refighting of the Great

Game that had pitted the West, led by Great Britain, against the Russians in the nineteenth century.

In the Oval Office, National Security Advisor Ross Conejo brought the Archipelago strategy home to the president by placing pins in locations on a large globe that had been brought into the room. One pin had been placed in North Africa, driven into the heart of Libya. Another pin had been placed in the southern Philippines, the so-called "Wild South" that was a hotbed of political unrest and endemic, chaotic low-intensity warfare.

Conejo had placed a third pin in a region of the Azerbaijani republic known as Nagorno-Karabakh. Yet another pin was inserted into the Amazonia Rectangle, a roughly box-shaped area encompassing the borders of Colombia, Ecuador, and Brazil, where U.S. counter-insurgency troops were currently campaigning.

Still other pins marking other developing trouble spots joined those already inserted into the surface of the globe.

"Mr. President, connect the data points—connect the dots—and you will see the invisible made visible," declared the National Security Advisor. "You will see the Archipelago of Terror that forms an invisible state. The neo-Soviets want this state to exist in order to weaken the West and attack at the pressure points—the fault lines of civilization, if you will."

The president nodded. Conejo's graphic demonstration had been clear; it had made a believer out of him.

But what nobody in the Oval Office understood at that moment was that there were two other data points—stretching some three thousand miles across a vast expanse of open ocean—that even Conejo's incisive analysis of the global threat had failed to identify.

Soon they would know about this hidden threat, too, and to their consternation because of their having neglected to detect it. For the moment, they were too focused on Libya to see that the storm was coming.

Commander Butcher saw the secure telex confirm in written form the orders that he had just received from CINCMED a few minutes before. Those orders were to launch fighter aircraft to test the resolve of the Libyans. The aircraft would undertake airborne exercises that would bring them over the Gulf of Sirte, crossing the Libyan's proclaimed Zone of Death in the process.

F-35 Joint Strike Fighters would be launched

from the deck of the carrier. Any Libyan aircraft were to be annihilated should they try to interfere in the U.S. fleet exercises.

The commander relayed these orders to his exec. Battle lines were now drawn. The combatants were engaged. The United States was at the brink of war, and there was no going back.

chapter *eight*

While Marines of Force One were slogging through the jungles of Amazonia, other elements of the go-anywhere, do-anything combat brigade were engaged in missions in far-flung corners of the globe. The data points that marked the islands of the invisible archipelago described by NSA Ross Conejo in the Oval Office were under assault by military forces in an attempt to stem the terrorist malignancies before they could grow and spread.

In the southern Philippines, the island of Mindanao and surrounding isles in the Philippine Sea marked the sites of entrenched insurgent forces. In the midst of this chain of jungle bases was an outcropping of densely forested rock called Rojang Island. The island had become the stronghold of well-equipped troops trained by neo-Sov experts in low-intensity warfare.

In the preceding eight months, U.S. orbital surveillance PHOTINT sensors had registered high-quality images of Soviet freighters out of the Aral Sea port of Aral'sk landing at the island and delivering stocks of military equipment, including spares and Soviet training personnel. The freighters disgorged stockpiles of war materiél from small arms to SAM transporters as well as ammunition and spares for all combat systems.

Despite the presence of U.S. naval forces in the littoral waters of the Philippine Sea, which subjected the island to TLAM strikes and to sorties by carrier-based F-35s and F/A-18s, a defensive network of pillboxes, blockhouses, and cave fortifications had been successfully established by the forces on the island.

A network of transmitter towers was a cause of dismay when it was discovered that this was a crude but effective counterstealth radar system linked by underground fiber-optic cables to control nodes scattered throughout the island. Surface-to-air missile installations ringed Rojang Island as well. These SAMs were advanced variants equipped with countersteallth tracking capability, enabling them to pose a significant threat to first-line U.S. and coalition fighter aircraft, such as the JSF and Raptor, as well as the aging though still formidable F-117A and B-2.

The question of what point there was to putting all of this defensive infrastructure in a remote corner of the Philippine Sea occurred to Pentagon military analysts. The answer wasn't in the end all that surprising, but it came as a shock nonetheless. The nexus of terror was using Rojang as a development center and testing ground for chemical and biological weaponry. It wasn't just anthrax that was being produced here but also delivery systems that would enable targeting of large population centers.

Rojang Island was in many way the Chernobyl of the Philippines.

Admiral Hallseye stood on the bridge of the USS *Ronald Reagan*, a Ticonderoga-class-cruiser. Officially, the nerve center of the carrier battlegroup assembled in the Philippine Sea was the carrier *William Jefferson Clinton*. Commissioned in 2008, the *Clinton* was a low-observable supercarrier optimized for combat in littoral waters. Unofficially, Hallseye had delegated command and control to his exec, Rear Admiral Quentin Collins, who occupied the command chair of the *Clinton*'s combat information center.

Hallseye was the kind of commander who believed in getting as close to the heat and grind of combat as possible. His epitome of a naval commander was Nelson, and he had tried to live up to that legend's career accomplishments. Hallseye clamped the stump of a soggy and long-dead cigar in the side of his teeth and raised the binoculars to his face.

By his side stood the skipper of the cruiser, Commander John Bonar, Marine Major General Prentice Truebland, who was to command the U.S. Marines about to land on Rojang Island, and Commander James Ring, who commanded the units of Her Majesty's Royal Marines, who were jointly attacking the island with their U.S. allies.

Through the lenses of his binoculars, Hallseye scanned the beachheads where in only a short time contingents of Marines would stage a from-the-sea landing under ferocious battle conditions. Once again the Marines would be tested in combat to take and hold a dangerous objective in the Pacific. Amplified by digital circuitry, Hallseye beheld what he surmised was a lethal gauntlet awaiting U.S. and British troops about to hit the beaches.

As always, the Marines would be the first troops

in and the last troops out. Spearheading the joint U.S.-U.K. force would be Marine Force One. A battalion-sized element of the elite USMC brigade had been assembled, trained, and equipped for the rugged conditions of the mission.

The brigade's commander, Lieutenant Colonel David Saxon, was with the troops assembled aboard the *Clinton*. Saxon would lead a special light detachment of company strength toward a critical objective of the mission. All the members of the assembled invasion force awaited Hallseye's orders to assault the island and storm the beachheads.

Beside Hallseye, Commander Ring had also completed a scan of the beach zone and the mountainous country lying beyond the cliffs facing the strip of volcanic sand between them and the sea.

"I'm confident we can do this," said Ring. "There's the possibility of it costing us, but I'm confident. Bloody awful mess it would have been last time around, though."

"Yeah, I was thinking the same thing," said Hallseye. "This is a fifth-generation military force ready to attack. Damn far cry from what our grandfathers had to deal with at places like Saipan or Iwo Jima."

Ring nodded.

"Nick," Hallseye addressed his aide aboard the cruiser, "double check with the *Clinton*'s CIC.

Weather and ground conditions. State of readiness. The whole shot. I want to know if we're good to go."

"Yes, sir."

Hallseye's aide opened his laptop and consulted the operational database, which was constantly updated with the latest combat information. This data was culled from a multitude of land, sea, air, space, and intelligence assets that produced a comprehensive picture of the strategic and tactical situation. The aide called up the CIC of the *Clinton* on secure videoconference link, and Hallseye was able to consult with his XO in the CIC.

"My forces are ready to go, John," he said to his British colleague when he'd completed his checks.

"We're ready, too," replied the Royal Marines commander. "This is the moment."

Hallseye nodded. He turned to his XO as the wind drove spray across the bridge of the cruiser.

"This is it. We're going in," he said.

Hallseye jutted his chin at the other vessels in the task force.

"Tell 'em."

Some three thousand miles away from joint U.S.-U.K. fleet ops in the Philippine Sea and some two hundred miles inshore from the Mediterranean, two other warriors were also preparing for battle under considerably different circumstances.

Yevgeny Petrovich and Nikita Malik were in the cockpits of advanced technology fighters. The planes were conducting combat exercises in the remote reaches of the Libyan desert, a region of desolation that stretches some thousand miles between the shores of Tripoli and the marshlands that divide the North African nation that was once, long ago, the city state of Carthage, from the veldt and jungles of equatorial Africa.

The planes scudded over the desert rises and declivities, leaving exhaust contrails in their wake. As they performed high-speed maneuvers they were tracked through binoculars by ground-based human observers and by millimeter-wave radar using computerized machinery. High-speed cameras linked to those radars and computer systems followed their every move. The aircraft were also under observation by Soviet imaging satellites in orbit high above the earth.

Other Soviet space assets, including far stealtheir and more highly maneuverable satellites than the imaging types, were part of an elaborate surveillance and reconnaissance network that kept tabs on U.S. and coalition spy systems in orbit and in the regional theater. For decades, the Soviets had allocated huge military expenditures toward stealth research. It had paid off in a system that allowed the Sovs to spy on U.S. spy satellites while these sought to spy on ground-based targets.

The air exercises that were taking place over the Libyan desert proving grounds were assured of secrecy because of the Soviet surveillance and reconnaissance countermeasures network. The Soviet Stavka, the equivalent of the U.S. Joint Chiefs of Staff, had assured the Libyan air force that it could conduct operations safe from hostile observation for several hours on this particular morning within the perimeter of the secret proving grounds. As the planes went through their aerial maneuvers, the skies overhead were constantly scanned by Russian space assets to make sure that operational secrecy was maintained.

The planes were the reason for this complicated arrangement. The two jets were the finest the Soviet aerospace industry had ever produced. In silhouette, the Berkuts presented a radical departure in fighter aircraft design with their swept-forward wings, nose canards, and tailplane control surface arrays. They looked like nothing Western aviation had produced. Beyond mere appearances, the planes' entire design philosophy was considerably different than what U.S. aerospace firms had built into the nation's warplanes.

Like all Soviet aircraft, the Berkuts were capable of delivering raw power and speed. That was expected. What was unexpected was the high level of stealthiness that the Soviets had incorporated into the design of these advanced technology fighters. More powerful than their Western counterparts and capable of longer operational flight ranges, the Berkuts were also almost as stealthy as the F-22 Raptor, by far the stealthiest fighter in the world's aircraft inventories.

Possessing both power and stealth, the Berkut was more than a match for the frontline fighters flown by the U.S. The reason for the great secrecy surrounding the present flight exercises was that Al-Sharq had pulled a magnificent coup by acquiring the Berkuts. He now had at his disposal two of the finest fighter aircraft in the world. The Libyan leader was determined to keep this secret until the moment came to use his new warplanes in combat.

It made no difference that Soviet pilots flew these two planes, or that the export versions with which Tripoli was supplied were somewhat stripped-down models of indigenous Soviet versions. The main thing was that Libya now possessed a rapid, long-range strike capability that could challenge the Americans and prevail.

The Shark of Tripoli knew that the Soviets were

intent on eventually making similar export versions of the Berkut the world's premier aircraft to challenge and replace American Joint Strike Fighters, which were the standard fighters flown by most of the world's nations. In staging a confrontation with the U.S. fleet, Al-Sharq was well aware that the Kremlin was using him as its stalking horse and as a lightning rod to draw fire from the U.S. None of this mattered to the Libyan honcho.

In the dogfight between U.S. Navy F-35s and his Soviet-supplied Berkuts, the Shark of Tripoli would be the Kremlin's agent in pitting the Berkut against the best frontline fighter in the world. If the Berkut won the challenge, then his Soviet patrons would reap untold billions in hard currency sales from global clients.

At the same time, the Shark's prestige in the Third and Arab worlds would rise, and he would reap renewed benefits from the Soviets. If the Libyan dictator failed, however, the outcome would be the reverse. It would spell disaster for the Father Colonel and his government. If his own people or the Americans would not oust him, then a Soviet-sponsored coup certainly might. The Libyan commander knew that everything turned on this gambit. It was all or nothing.

What Al-Sharq was not aware of was what was

taking place inside the head of one of the pilots of the two Berkut aircraft. Strapped down into the pilot's form-fitted seat while he performed high g-loaded maneuvers, the pilot executed a flawless reverse Immelmann and came up behind one of the old Mig-29s that the two advanced technology fighters were chasing in the high-speed combat exercise.

Only the pilots of the Berkuts knew that they would be firing live ammunition and armed missiles. The Libyans who piloted the MiGs had been informed that strikes on their planes would be recorded by laser paints in exercise mode. Al-Sharq had personally signed the secret orders that would virtually insure the deaths of the MiG pilots, who believed themselves Libyan patriots.

At standoff range, the Berkut pilot got a good skin paint on the hot exhaust gases exiting the older MiG's twin exhaust nacelles. The advanced Giatsint missiles carried in the internal weapons bay of the Berkut homed in on multiple target signatures in addition to IR, so the missile that he launched would almost inevitably find its mark no matter what, but heat was still the most reliable targeting signature and the easiest one to lock onto.

Predictably, the MiG pilot began evasive maneuvers once alerted by his plane's threat-warning radar. The pilot of the Berkut saw him execute a superbly timed wingover and half-Immelmann that was textbook perfect. Such a shame, he thought. The target plane's pilot was damn good. He shouldn't have been wasted like this.

But he was doomed just the same. Especially when the Berkut pilot's wingman fired his own missile at the escaping MiG, which was now flying evasive maneuvers down on the deck, only a few score yards above the undulating surface of the sun-baked desert. Such maneuvers were designed to break radar-lock on the escaping plane amid the ground clutter of reflecting radar lobes and make it fade into the thermal background of the desert below; and these tactics ordinarily stood a good chance of working.

In the case of the two missiles fired by the Berkuts, though, the MiG didn't have a chance. The advanced AAMs been specially designed to filter out background clutter and countermeasures—such as the chaff clouds that were now being ejected by the desperately fleeing MiG—and unerringly close on their target at supersonic velocities. The MiG's fate was sealed as the first of the two AAMs streaked up the plane's left exhaust nacelle a second before the second missile collided with the fuselage just aft of the MiG's left wing-root.

Twin fireballs mushroomed from the stricken

plane. The pilot ejected safely, and the pilots of the two chase planes watched pieces of the stricken MiG's cockpit canopy break away in spinning chunks of glass and metal as the target jet blew apart, and its burning, smoldering remnants pin-wheeled down to the desert sands below.

The pilot in the Berkut who had fired the first missile was glad that they'd seen the pilot safely eject. He hoped his former adversary survived the encounter.

His finger hovered over the flashing button that would fire another missile at the second MiG, then he drew it back.

"Let the other plane go," he told his wingman.

"Affirmative."

The Russian pilot had no great love for Libya, but he recognized a kindred spirit and a brave soldier in the actions of the Libyan combat pilot. If he were not executed by Libyan hit squads to silence him, the fighter jock would probably be cursing his leader right now, for by this time he must know that he had been set up as a live target for superior airborne forces.

The Russian pilot wondered—as he executed a wingover and performed a powered descent to return to the landing strip for refueling, maintenance by ground crew, and post-exercise debriefing—what the

Libyan would think if he knew that one of the two Russians who had fired on him was planning to defect to the West with the Berkut he was flying as his ticket to asylum. The pilot had already been in backchannel contact with CIA assets who were waiting to spirit him to the West.

All they wanted was the plane. It would be a small price to pay for having bought his freedom from Soviet Russia forever.

chapter *nine*

The attack on Rojang Island commenced at 0520 hours (Lima).

Rising columns of smoke and isolated fires marked the places where Tomahawk cruise missile strikes had assailed targets in the preparation attacks from war planes and offshore naval vessels.

More TLAM strikes and fighter bombing runs were continuing to reduce targets in the battle zone as amphibious troops began a fast-moving effort to take the beaches. The thunder of multiple explosions boomed and rolled across land, sea, and air. Navy JSFs and FA/18 Super Hornets streaked back out of the billowing smoke of battle, roaring over the heads of oncoming troops at supersonic speeds.

As targets inland were continually reduced by coordinated offshore fires, U.S. and Royal Marines were on their way to their designated beach landing zones. There were three beaches in all, each separated into two zones. Beach Red was a British beachhead. Beach Yellow was an American venture. Beach Gold was a joint venture with British and U.S. Marine forces, each tasked with taking and holding east and west corners of the beach landing zone.

The leathernecks came charging in from the sea and through the air. They came in on LCACs, fleet air cushion vehicles that skimmed the surface of the ocean at high speeds. Equipped with machine guns and rocket launchers, the LCACs assaulted the beachheads firing their weapons. The amphibious hovercraft made the transition from over-water movement to over-land locomotion without a hitch. They sped inland, ferrying the troops to forward battle areas on the beach zones.

The Marines also rushed to join the battle via V-22 Osprey convertiplanes. The Ospreys, which could ferry a company of troops including equipment and weapons to their landing zones, had risen straight up from the decks of ships offshore. Once at their thirty-foot translation altitude, their engines had rotated into a horizontal position, enabling the aircraft to function as conventional prop-driven aircraft.

Marine Whiskey Cobra gunships flew combat security missions for the V-22. The nimble yet heavily armed helicopters could get in close and work the battlefield with rockets and heavy-caliber gunfire. The Cobras could see what was happening up close and suppress targets on the ground, such as machine-gun emplacements that would be hard to detect and destroy by any other available methods.

As the Ospreys loitered or were in transit to their LZs, the Cobras came scooting in to conduct battlefield reconnaissance. Manned by a pilot and weapon systems officer, who sat forward of the snake driver in the lower cockpit, the Cobras picked out hostile targets that were waiting to destroy inbound forces.

The tactic helped smoke out numerous targets that were well-hidden or too small to see from the air yet would have spelled a lot of trouble for arriving troop carrier airships. Some of these targets ran from well-hidden heavy machine-gun emplacements and mobile SAMs to shell holes or caves from which enemy troops could pop up and launch a shoulder-fired missile at the Ospreys or rake them with small-arms fire.

When they found unfriendlies below, the Cobras would go into action. Bigger targets were taken down with heavier weapons, such as Hellfire or TOW missiles. These weapons were carried on launch rails bristling from the stub wings that projected from the Cobras' sides. When the WSO sitting up front got a fix on the threat below, the missiles were launched, vectoring down on contrails of smoke to destroy the ground-based threats.

If smaller targets were detected, the weapons system officer might decide to rake the bad guys with bullets fired from the tri-barelled M197 twenty-millimeter cannon mounted under the fuselage chin. The cannon was slaved to the shooter's helmet, and the gun turret could be swung from side to side to bring fire where needed by movements of the WSO's head.

Once the landing zones were prepared, the Ospreys began to come in, hover, and land their troops. Marines came out of the rear of the Ospreys shouting war cries and hitting the ground running.

Many were able to move to positions of concealment on the fringes of the landing zones. Others immediately came under fire from hidden enemy troops that had survived the scathing assaults from long-range missiles and in-close AH-1W gunship attacks.

Men fell where they ran, cut down by bullets that raked their midsections with ragged puncture lines. Others dragged wounded buddies to the safety of shell holes or the cover of the shattered wreckage of enemy blockhouses and pillboxes that had been destroyed in earlier attacks. Still others ran on, engaging the enemy at close quarters with small-arms fire and fixed bayonets.

All over the knob of volcanic rock projecting from the whitecapped seas off the coast of the southern Philippines, the Marines were landing, taking ground, and consolidating their assigned beachheads.

In the first hour of the assault, the lightning-swift series of coordinated attacks enabled friendly forces to secure an ever-widening cordon of control over the island. The Marines had come to stay this time, as they had done so many times before.

Halfway around the world, several miles off the Mediterranean coast of North Africa, the U.S. Sixth Fleet lay at anchor. Meteorologically, the weather was fair and calm. Politically, there were thunderclouds gathering. Overhead surveillance assets, from SR-71 Blackbirds to intelligence-gathering satellites, parked in geosynchronous earth orbit, had collected the disturbing data that the Libyans were making preparations to launch an attack on U.S. naval forces.

Equipped with Sovremmeny-class frigates from Russian shipyards, Al-Sharq, the Father Colonel, was suspected to be preparing for war against the Americans. There was good reason for this supposition. Intelligence assessments indicated that the Libyans were under pressure from their patrons in Moscow to use the sophisticated military hardware with which they'd been supplied.

The goal would be to attack U.S. naval forces asymmetrically, using stealthy missiles fired by the Sovremmeny ships to destroy much larger American vessels. This tactic had sunk three British ships during the Falklands War. A year later, during the reflagging operation for oil tankers in the Persian Gulf that became known as the Tanker War, the same basic strategy was responsible for blowing a huge hole in the starboard flank of the USS *Stark*.

"A similar outcome in our present situation could strike a devastating blow against the Americans, resulting in their withdrawal from the Sacred Waters."

The speaker was General Omar Suled, the Father Colonel's military chief of staff. The scene was the presidential palace in Tripoli, where the General Council of War, a strategic planning body made up of the Leader's closest political and military advisers, had convened to determine the course to take in the face of the American offshore presence.

"The Americans are an inconsistent people," Suled went on. "But on this one point they are always predictable: they will turn and run when enough pressure is put on them. Send one of their carriers to the bottom of the Mediterranean, and the survivors will sail for home."

"Yes," the Leader replied. "And then they will do to this very chamber in which we now sit, and to the building in which this chamber lies, and to the bunker system deep beneath it, and to countless other targets in Libya precisely what they did to Iraq in their campaign of shock and awe."

Suleh would not be swayed, despite his leader's censure.

"There are considerable differences," he pressed on. His head turned this way and that to allow his gaze to bore into the eyes of those seated at the council table. "The Soviets were then in disarray, and the Iraqis were strategically isolated. Today the situation has reversed itself. The Russian bear is again a force to be reckoned with. The Americans will shrink from a confrontation. I am convinced of this."

"Perhaps our comrade general overstates his case," declared Minister of State Saidal Fagih, the flesh above his aquiline nose wrinkling as he spoke, as if he had smelled something foul in the air. "The Soviet Union may have been reconstituted, but we dare not convince ourselves that Cold War logic applies. It was the threat of escalation to nuclear war that underlay everything then. The U.S. National Missile Defense and many other developments argue that the Americans might well not flinch from confronting the Reds today."

Seated at the head of the long table, his eyes shrouded behind the dark-tinted lenses of his aviator glasses, his face darkened beneath the visor of his billed military cap, Al-Sharq, the Father Colonel, nodded faintly. Before anyone else could speak to voice an opinion, he held up his hand. The room, silent before, now reached another level of silence.

"You have all spoken your hearts and your minds. The counsels you have voiced have been noted." He paused and regarded all of the assembled cabinet. A small smile flickered on his lips. "I have decided that we will first test the Americans' resolve."

The Father Colonel asked all except his chief military advisers to leave the chamber. There was much to be discussed.

The Colombian hill town of Ochos Cruces was nestled at an altitude of thirty thousand feet, high amid the thin air of the Andes Mountain range. Ochos Cruces was currently in the hands of Evangelista insurgent forces. The partisans had staged numerous attacks on U.S. formations in the rugged high country surrounding the village.

Ochos Cruces might have been bypassed by the U.S. Marines except for the fact that it commanded a vantage point over an important valley system. It had been from here that the Evangelistas had posted spotters armed with high-powered binoculars and telescopes.

The clear, thin, dust-free air at that altitude was the perfect medium for observation of distant troop movements. The observation post was the reason for accurate enemy targeting of U.S. ground forces working the valley system to search out and destroy *guerillero* bases, hidden airstrips, and the underground tunnel systems that often connected them.

The time was 0500 hours. The night, or what was left of it, was moonless. The weather was clear. A Marine patrol threaded its way up the narrow mountain trail. There was a lizard in the jungle that had a peculiar mating call. The mating call sounded like, "Fuck You Fuck You Fuck You."

When asked about this, the natives told the Marines that the lizards made this sound at this time of year only. The Marines predictably called the reptile the "Fuck-You Lizard." Its call was not loved by them. The troopers heard the call tonight as the column moved up the side of the mountain.

The call was also heard by insurgent forces that waited in the dark silent town. The townspeople had either fled to the safety of neighboring villages and forested regions or were hunkered in basements waiting until the shooting commenced and stopped.

The Marines entered the town and began house-to-house operations. Their intention was to secure the town, round up insurgent forces, take all captured Evangelista rebels prisoner, and establish a forward area command post and observation point in the town.

They were not destined to have a cakewalk in their efforts to secure this particular village.

All of a sudden, fire began breaking out from the rooftops, from the streets, from seemingly everywhere at once. Marines found themselves caught in multiple crossfires. They found themselves embroiled in a furball from hell.

"Paint the target!"

The gunnery sergeant's orders were immediately obeyed by the crew of the fast attack vehicle he commanded. The Stryker light-armored vehicle took several hits from small-arms fire but the steel-jacketed bullets didn't pierce its well-protected hull. The Stryker was protected against heavier weapons, too, but there were limits to its survivability. Its best defense was its speed and maneuverability, two survival options that weren't readily available in the confined quarters of the narrow street.

The other option was to use the Stryker's TOW missile launcher mounted atop the vehicle to take out the source of the fire. This happened to be a stone house at the top of the street, on which the Marines could see two Evangelista rebels crouching and getting ready to fire an RPG round at the armored vehicle.

"Go!"

The Stryker fired its TOW before the partisan with the RPG could get off his shot. The heat-seeking missile left the launch rails trailing its guidance cable. The shooter inside the armored war wagon watched its progress through his scope, correcting course by means of hand-grip controls inside the vehicle.

"Go, bitch, go!"

Three seconds to impact. The TOW sped through the air. Two seconds to impact. The image on the console screen filled the field of view.

Impact.

The TOW missile's warhead struck its target with the tremendous force of transferred kinetic energy. Its shaped-charge high-explosive warhead detonated in a sunball of fire. The blast disintegrated the front of the house and blew to bits everything at the point of detonation. This included the two *guerillero* shooters who were about to launch their RPG strikes against the armored vehicle.

The Stryker rolled toward the smoking wreckage where tongues of yellow flame licked upward from fires inside. The entire building was now ablaze. The commander got topside and looked around, using what tankers like to call their "top vision."

The scene of carnage was even starker in real life. He climbed behind the 7.62 millimeter MAG machine gun mounted on a pintle stand atop the Stryker, charged the weapon, and raked the front of the house with bullets. Tracers, spaced every third round, gleamed phosphorescent white as they streaked down into the burning building.

Suddenly there was a tremendous explosion. The blast wave hit the tank commander before his eardrums were assaulted by the fierce concussion. He was almost thrown clear of the Stryker's hatch by the enormous force of the blast.

The next thing the sergeant knew, he awoke in a field hospital. The doctors told him he'd be okay. There'd been a huge cache of ammunition and explosives hidden inside the house. When he'd raked the place with white hot tracers, he'd set off the entire arms stockpile.

"Damn near killed you," he was told by the group of Marine physicians attending him as he lay on his hospital bed.

The doctors finished with him and then walked down the ward and went to another cot. The commander looked over to where they went out of nothing more than idle curiosity.

The guy lying there looked just like a mummy. He was bandaged from head to foot. The sergeant, who'd been knocked unconscious by the blast from the arms cache in the blazing house, turned his head and stared at the ceiling.

Guess I was *lucky*, he thought.

chapter *ten*

The *King Albert III* tooted its horn twice to announce its imminent departure. Then the huge ship slid from its berth. Onboard were hundreds of guests and scores of crew. The enormous cruise vessel had departed the Aruba pier promptly at nine A.M. on a Sunday morning. It was scheduled to reach international waters by mid-morning. From there it would sail a northeastward course that would first cross the West Indies, and then bring it into South Atlantic waters.

Two days later, when the *King Albert III* reached the Azores, it would turn twenty degrees to the south and steam toward Gibraltar in order to make its passage into the Mediterranean Sea. The entire trip was scheduled to take five days.

By midnight on the first day of sailing, the ocean liner had crossed the southernmost island of the Mariannas group that marked the southernmost point of the West Indies chain. The cruise ship crossed into South Atlantic waters at approximately half past the hour.

Passengers onboard were engaged in a variety of activities. In the largest of the liner's three ballrooms, a dance contest was being held. In the smallest of the ballrooms, which was being used as a lounge and dining area, scores of passengers were still sitting down to the final courses of a late-night supper.

A comedian, advertised as having last played the Sands on the Las Vegas strip, was winding down a tired monologue. He got a few laughs for his trouble. The crowd had heard it all before. The middle-sized ballroom was closed down as it had nothing scheduled that night.

In the staterooms that lined the corridors of the vast cruise ship, many passengers were already asleep. In the operations center perched high above the forward deck of the ocean liner, the captain was still at his post, though he would soon be relieved by his exec when he went off duty.

Captain Trevor Reese-Mogg was a twenty-two-year veteran of the cruise-line industry. Prior to having been given his commission to serve as the first captain of the brand-new *King Albert III*, Reese-Mogg had been captain of the *Queen Mary II*.

Before that Reese-Mogg had commanded a British frigate, HMS *Redoubtable*, in the Falklands War. The *Redoubtable* had been sunk by an Argentine Exocet missile. Reese-Mogg had lost half his crew in the night attack. He still had nightmares concerning the action. After the war in the Falklands was over, Reese-Mogg resigned his commission with the Royal Navy and entered commercial service.

Tonight, as was Reese-Mogg's habit, he toured the operational decks of the ship before retiring to his quarters for a few hours of rest. Reese-Mogg was liked by the crew, who knew him to be as capable as he was good-natured. On this voyage, though, they sensed that something had changed.

More to the point, the crew sensed that something was wrong with their captain. Ever since the ocean liner's debarkation from its last port of call, the Spanish coastal town of Costa Blancas, Reese-Mogg's normally lean face had grown even gaunter and paler than usual.

The captain's manner had changed, too. Although he was still solicitous of his crew, and as approachable and good-humored as ever, there was a kind of brooding temper that had fallen over him. A rumor had been going around the ship that Reese-Mogg spent his nights drinking, alone in his cabin, that there was something he wanted to forget.

All the same, as Reese-Mogg made his usual rounds of the operational areas of the deck tonight, the tall, imposing figure of the captain seemed as much in command as usual. Reese-Mogg paused on the bridge and checked weather radar, sonar, emergency radio channels, GPS, and other satcom channels. He spoke with the helmsman on night duty concerning the course that had been plotted. He reviewed the night's security schedule with the chief duty officer.

The ocean liner's amiable captain ended his tour by wishing the crewmen on the bridge a good night and left for his quarters, adding his customary admonition to wake him if even the smallest matter seemed to require his attention.

Reese-Mogg closed the door to his cabin behind him and locked it. He stripped to his shorts and poured himself a nightcap of cured malt liquor. It was a bonded Scottish blend that he favored. Reese-Mogg sipped the whiskey and set the glass down on a nightstand. Then, from the top drawer, he took a nine-millimeter Glock semiautomatic pistol.

For a few minutes he looked at the weapon. He had loaded it the night before, and the red indicator was showing at the top of the slide to indicate that a round was chambered. Reese-Mogg smiled as his eyes ran up and down the length of the pistol barrel. He then took the weapon and placed it in his mouth.

Reese-Mogg felt the cold impression made by the hard ring of metal against the top of his palate. The sharp bite of the cold quickly vanished, but he could still feel the pressure of the muzzle against the roof of his mouth. Before he thought too much about the closeness of the muzzle to the stem of his brain, and about what would happen after a trigger pull sent the hollow-nosed round tearing through bone and tissue, he squeezed the trigger.

The companionway was empty, and the round had been custom loaded to fire at near subsonic velocity. In addition to this, the captain's mouth and head had acted as a natural baffle system for the report of the bullet.

The hollow-point nose round fragmented as it tore through soft tissue and cranial bone. Most of the fragments ripped apart the interior of the captain's skull. Others ricocheted down and exited his nose, throat, neck, and upper torso. A soaking exit wound pumped out spurts of dark arterial blood as his body sank to the floor.

The captain's corpse would lay there for many hours more until it was at last discovered.

In one of the plush state rooms on the upper deck, the couple that had vacationed at the Villa Marengo in Aruba were enjoying a late-night bottle of chilled champagne in the lavish suite's Norwegian hot tub. Both were completely nude. The woman leaned back and let the man do things to her that he did extremely well and were the sole reasons why she had selected him as her companion on this voyage.

Her name was Heather Hunnicut, and she was the wife of the U.S. secretary of state, Warren Hunnicut. The man who was now doing the things she found so enjoyable, except from a different angle than he had been doing them a few minutes before, was a former Spanish lounge singer.

Heather Hunnicut was aware of this but not that he was also an agent of the Nexus. At the moment, she could not have cared less if he were from Mars, though. She was having too good a time as she moved her nipples back and forth, brushing his mustache and lips. Then, with a laugh, she sank below the waters, putting her breasts to other uses.

FROM THE HALLS OF MONTEZUMA

Between the broad northern shoreline of Venezuela and the West Indies there can be found numerous sea caves, coves, islets, grottos, and desolate stretches of beach.

In all of these, and in the mountainous jungle regions that lie beyond the strips of sand girdling the warm, placid waters of that southern stretch of the Atlantic long known to sailors as the Sargasso Sea, few travelers will venture. These are remote, undeveloped places, home to sea birds and turtles, with scant signs of permanent human habitation.

As a result, this region of sea and land has long been a safe haven for pirates, and not only for the buccaneers of centuries past. Hard men with fast boats today work these shores and the waters around them.

Many of them are smugglers. They earn their living making runs along the coastline of Brazil.

Others, with larger boats and more powerful engines, will make the thousand-mile transatlantic run to Africa. In this way, drugs, cigarettes, digital electronics, small arms, and even more exotic contraband flows with regularity between three continents.

Still other seafarers who inhabit the coastal regions between Venezuela and the Indies are latter-day pirates in every sense of the word. Their boats, while fast, are also heavily gunned. Their crews are captained by hard, cold men who care less for human life than other men might care for the life of an insect.

Their crews are equally ferocious. They are taken from the ranks of the downtrodden, the impoverished, and the hopeless. They come from the slums of Rio De Janeiro, where shantytowns are breeding grounds for drug addiction and hatred. They come from Caracas, with slums almost as bad as those of Rio. They come from across the South Atlantic, from islands off the coast of west Africa, or from the continent itself, whose war-torn west coast is also a breeding ground for violence and crime, and where only those with no scruples stand a chance of surviving to grow to manhood.

Like the buccaneers in whose footsteps they follow, they form an army of psychopathic raiders who take no hostages and kill their victims with relish. Yachts sailing these waters have long carried weapons—and hired crewmen who know how to use them—because to traverse these seas unarmed is to invite death in the night. Yet even weapons are no guarantee against attack and boarding. The pirates who work the waters off the Venezuelan coast are armed with technological aids, massive firepower, and boats with specially silenced engines.

When a prize on the high seas is taken, the chain

of events follows a generally predictable course. First, the crew and passengers of the captured vessel are rounded up. They are forced to turn over their cash and valuables. After being looted the men are killed. The women are raped. Afterward, the women too are killed.

Once the sea has claimed the bodies of the pirates' victims, anything else of value is taken aboard the raiding vessel. The captured boat or ship is then scuttled and sent to the bottom. Many a yacht has simply vanished in this way, never to be found again.

Among the most notorious of contemporary pirates who prowl this region was one known as O'Finnegan. Visitors had come to his encampment two days before. They were expected. O'Finnegan had been doing business with their leader for years.

They were partners, partners of long-standing. O'Finnegan, a pirate, made no bones or pretensions about what he did for a living. He robbed people, killed them, ran guns, whiskey, drugs, anything that went for a dollar. His partner was of a different stripe. He proclaimed himself a revolutionary, a philosopher, a freedom fighter, a poet, a champion of the rights of the oppressed.

Neither of the two, pirate nor revolutionary, was

exactly what they seemed. Both went back a long time. Yet while their origins lay in the same place, and what had come between was scattered and diffuse, what was to follow would link them together again in an adventure destined to exceed all that had come before.

On the bridge of the giant ocean liner, the night crew had settled in for an uneventful passage of the waters of the south Atlantic. An assortment of innovations in communications and navigational aids insured that the cruise vessel sailed a true and straight course with speed and safety.

In addition to sonar, the ship also had a real-time downlink to a French synthetic aperture radar satellite parked in geostationary orbit. The SAR imagery produced accurate, high-resolution data on any obstructions that might lie in the path of the liner as she made way across the darkened seas. Unlike conventional photo imaging, SAR images also showed what might lie directly below the ocean's surface. Such innovations insured that there would be no more *Titanic*s striking icebergs ever again.

The *King Albert III* also had its own onboard suite of weather and tracking radars, their antennas shrouded and protected, beneath watertight domes and behind pods, against sea salt and harsh weather conditions. These radars were high-resolution millimeter wave types that could see outward to three hundred miles in any direction.

This type of radar was useful in giving the liner advance warning of the approach of other ships that might be on a collision course. It was just such a collision with another vessel that sank the *Andrea Doria* off the coast of New York City decades before.

The crew in the bridge was trained to monitor the equipment, and the equipment itself was programmed to issue warning messages in the event its computer processors detected the approach of vessels or the imminence of collision with natural objects, or, in the case of weather radar, the onset of a hurricane, gale, or other natural threat to the safety and smooth progress of the ship.

Should the computer system be infected with a virus, though, the picture might change. Had the crew manning the bridge that night discovered that their captain had committed a messy suicide in his cabin, then they might have been on the alert for trouble. Even so, they might not have suspected that the computer system of the liner had been virally infected and was not functioning according to their expectations.

After all, why would they have suspected that anything was amiss? A corpse, even the corpse of their captain, was one thing. In the absence of a "smoking gun," such as a computer disk in his pocket, there would have been no reason to make the conceptual leap toward a computer invasion.

And so the ocean liner sailed on, its automated digital systems keeping it steady on a course that was inching its way across the map toward the ship's ports of call on another continent still thousands of miles away.

The men on the vessel's bridge glanced at the monitors and instrumentation consoles from time to time as the night wore on. Occasionally a problem came up that required their attention. Most of the time nothing happened, and the watchstanders grew bored.

Sailors didn't control their ships anymore. Machines ran everything. Humans only watched. And at best, acted only when things started going seriously amiss.

The arrivals had rested in the sea cave by day, only awakening with the onset of the humid, moonless night. They were men as hard as the pirates who sailed and raided under the command of O'Finnegan.

Yet in many respects they were very different.

Their eyes blazed with a fanatical light. Their speech was littered with a baggage of phrases that held no meaning for men whose only goal in life was to plunder and kill.

Were they fools? wondered O'Finnegan. He didn't know, and he cared still less. He was only interested in carrying out this job. It was going to be his last one. His biggest. It would set him up for life.

"My friend, tonight we will begin an operation that will echo through the centuries," said the leader of the arrivals, clapping the pirate honcho on the back.

"I don't give a shit about your operation. You know that. I'm in this for the money. That and nothing else, compadre."

"You are . . . right now. But wait. Maybe things will change. They changed for me. You recall the time when we were both only interested in the one thing?"

"I remembered two, my friend," said O'Finnegan.

The other laughed.

"Yes," Carlos Evangelista told the pirate. "Two things. There is always the second, no? No matter what else, there is this second thing." The guerilla leader dragged on the cheroot held clenched between his teeth. Its tip glowed orange. "And yet it becomes as nothing. It is a trifle. So much of it have I had in the jungle, where the women will fuck a man for nothing, that it has grown to be of no importance."

"For me, compadre," said O'Finnegan, "it will always be a thing of importance. Of great importance."

"Well, I go to die," said the Evangelist. "There is nothing of more importance than to do this final thing before I meet my end. These *yanqui cabrones* have hunted me out of the jungle. The forces of repression have scored a temporary victory. But this thing we shall now do will even many a score. It is to be a terrible thing, but a thing of great beauty all the same. Hold such a thing against the other, *amigo*—I defy you tell me which is the better of the two things."

"Pussy is better," said O'Finnegan without a moment's hesitation.

Both men laughed.

Evangelista thought back to days long ago. The man known as O'Finnegan had been known as Carlos, then. Not the same Carlos who had been captured by the French and who still sits in a Parisian prison cell and who had drunk up the blood that had been spilled at a long-ago Olympic game like a jackal, the name he had been called for this obscene act. This O'Finnegan was the other Carlos, the first, called Carlos Marighella. He was a Brazilian, who was a thinker and a philosopher of global revolution.

Marighella's book, *The Mini Manual of the Urban Guerilla,* had fast become a classic terrorist handbook. Marighella had supposedly been gunned down in a fight with the police. But it had been a double who had actually died. The real Carlos had escaped, and he had then gone into another profession. Evangelista had been inspired by Carlos in his earlier years while in hiding from the Colombian army.

When he had learned that Carlos was still alive, Evangelista had begged him to join the fight in the jungle. O'Finnegan had not accepted the younger man's invitation. Yet they still enjoyed a close partnership. The rebel leader found that the pirate and smuggler was useful in bringing guns and ammunition in from across the sea and from places along the extensive coastline networks of the Americas.

"Anyway, it is good to be working together as one again," said the Evangelist to the man he admired.

"It's getting late," answered O'Finnegan curtly, not looking into the other man's eyes. "We'd better get going."

chapter *eleven*

He had known it was coming. Even so, he was stunned. The grueling weeks of practice on the remote desert range, the constant readiness for attack, had pointed to only a single conclusion: the Soviet-supplied Berkut stealth aircraft were soon to be called on to engage some target of major strategic importance.

Neither Yevgeny Petrovichn nor his wingman Nikita Malik had been informed of precisely what type of engagement the exercises were in preparation for. But there could be no doubt that something major was in the offing. When both stealth fighter pilots were summoned unexpectedly to a mission briefing, they knew that the moment was at hand.

Under the circumstances, they could not help but suspect that the new planes would be used in an attack on the U.S. carrier battlegroup in the Med. Yet such an attack, even if successful, would surely entail severe global repercussions. Petrovich had every confidence in the Berkuts. He knew professionally that the aircraft were equal, and in many respects superior, to the best flown by the Americans.

Still, using such warplanes in an engagement against the assembled might of a United States carrier group was to sow the wind and reap the whirlwind. Even if successful—which was highly probable, given the skills of the pilots and the capabilities of the first-line Russian planes—the fact remained that there were only two such planes on the Libyan side and many, many more on the side of the Americans.

The U.S., too, could field any number of other weapons in retaliation. The U.S. could strike back at Libya with long-range cruise missiles, unmanned aerial combat vehicles like Global Hawk, and with commando assaults anywhere in the country using Pave Low helicopters to deliver troops clandestinely to their targets. It could also overwhelm Libya's scant stealth aircraft resources by launching strikes using a panoply of stealth aircraft, from the B-2 bomber to new exotic transatmospheric planes that cruised at hypermach velocity.

What kind of idiots were these Libyans? wondered Petrovich. Moscow was in no danger of retaliation. The premier's policy had always been to select *poputchiki,* or puppets, to serve as surrogates for the Kremlin's war machine. If the *poputchiki* were successful, then further and more direct action might be contemplated, and then taken. Should the puppets fail, and they usually did, then Moscow would simply distance itself from their disgraced former client state and seek fresh opportunities elsewhere in the world.

Knowing all of this, and expecting that the orders he was awaiting would almost certainly be to carry out just such a suicidally stupid attack on U.S. forces, Petrovich was nonetheless stunned when his every expectation was confirmed.

"Gentlemen, you are called upon to launch a strike on the imperialists that will live on in the annals of history for a thousand years," said the Russian Air Force Colonel General, Feodor Tomachevsky, who was 10 Derzhinsky Square's liaison with the Libyans, after Libyan Air Force General

Ramad Barzoon had finished briefing the men in the mission.

"You two men must consider yourselves fortunate," Tomachevsky went on, while seated behind him Barzoon nodded with self-satisfaction, puffed up like a desert pigeon with inane pride.

"You have been chosen to carry out this mission. You have been chosen because you are the best. Not among the best, *tovarischi,* but the best beyond all doubt. You will be carrying nuclear weapons. You will sink the USS *Eisenhower*. The world will long talk about this."

Tomachevsky called for questions.

"Sir, I believe I may not have heard you correctly," Petrovich said in response. "Forgive me, sir, but my recollection is that you stated we would be staging a nuclear attack on the United States carrier group."

Tomachevsky did not falter, did not flinch, and did not smile. A cold malevolence came into his eyes. This question was not to have been asked, the look told the pilot; perhaps others, but not this. There was more meaning that could be read into that momentary look, too, Petrovich sensed. It might mean he would be replaced—meaning he would be killed and then replaced by a more pliable pilot.

The look departed as quickly as it had come into the general's eyes.

"Your hearing is excellent, Comrade Petrovich," said Tomachevsky. "And your understanding is entirely correct. You will be carrying Giatsint missiles armed with nuclear warheads. Our object is to sink the *Eisenhower* and as many of the other vessels as possible. Did you think that we would commit our finest pilots and our finest planes for a pissing contest?"

"No, sir. You are correct. I understand."

"Then you will carry out your orders without further questions or reservations. Assure me of this, or you will be removed from the mission."

"You have my assurance, general," said Petrovich. "I apologize for raising the question."

The general nodded but made no further response. The briefing was over. The pilots had their orders and were dismissed.

Petrovich could not see Tomachevsky's eyes fall heavily on the space between his shoulders as he left the room, but he thought he could feel them linger there for too long before the door shut behind him.

Petrovich returned to his quarters a troubled man. He wondered if General Tomachevsky had any inkling of what he had been planning. Who could say if they knew anyway and had permitted him to go this far for their own cunning reasons?

The pilot's quarters were spartan, even by the standards of the Russian air force, but were redeemed by panoramic views of the open desert that surrounded the military outpost. The Russian contingent that bivouacked at Al-Kamila air base had brought with them whatever comforts they could, and the Libyans were liberal in providing amenities such as vodka and caviar.

Petrovich got out a bottle of pepper vodka and a clean tumbler. He placed the glass on the writing desk beside the room's north-facing window, the one with the best view of the dunes and sky, and poured himself a generous slug of the clear alcohol. As was his habit, he drank it all in a single swallow. He would go easier on the rest.

As he poured and drank, Petrovich mentally went over the steps that had brought him to this point in time. Things had moved incredibly fast. Was it only something less than three months since he had been summoned to his commander's office on short notice?

Petrovich remembered climbing out of the cockpit of the Sukhoi fighter and being handed the orders to report immediately to Colonel Tomachevsky.

He was engaged in combat training exercises for the past week and was afraid that the call had something to do with his performance record.

This didn't make sense, since if there had been a problem with his performance he would have learned about it earlier and through other channels. Yet he had had no inkling about why he'd been summoned.

He learned why soon enough.

"Stand at ease, Captain," said the pilot's superior.

Rising from the desk, the officer had slowly regarded the pilot with a critical eye. Tomachevsky had earned the reputation as a no-nonsense staff officer, one prone to passing instant judgment that, once made, was never rescinded.

Petrovich cursed himself for not having changed into his dress uniform, but there had actually been no time. The orders he'd received had commanded his presence immediately. Knowing his commander, Petrovich took the word "immediately" literally. He feared that even a slight delay weighed against a more presentable appearance could find disfavor in Tomachevsky's eyes.

The colonel's stark appraisal went on for several long minutes. Then, to Petrovich's vast relief, the colonel uttered a single word.

"Sit."

Petrovich thanked the colonel and took the proferred chair. It faced the desk that Tomachevsky now again sat behind. Petrovich's relief was based on the perception that was he to have been dismissed or dressed down, it would have been done standing up. Petrovich's relief grew as Tomachevsky questioned him concerning his performance in flight exercises.

The dossier before the commander contained all relevant facts about the captain's professional and personal life. After his flurry of questions, Tomachevsky nodded to himself, his eyes fixed on the desk blotter. Then he looked up.

"You have been reassigned. Here are your orders."

Tomachevsky slid a sheet of paper across the desk.

"Prepare for departure to your new assignment. An Antonov is leaving at 0500 hours. You will be on it."

Tomachevsky half-rose and extended his hand across the desk.

Petrovich grasped it and shook. It felt oddly clammy.

"Thank you, sir," he said. Then he rose, saluted, and left.

The orders themselves were cryptic. They informed Petrovich that he was being reassigned to a flight-testing facility deep in the Urals, and that he was to receive further instructions upon arrival. The orders added that he was to discuss the reassignment with no one until he was given permission. This included his closest personal relations. He was on the plane within hours.

Petrovich refilled his glass. The vodka had brought on its expected sense of reverie. He drank again. Outside the window a dust storm had blown up, a constant weather phenomenon in this desert region that one learned to live with. The swirl of dust obscured the sky in a curtain of whirling wind-blown particles. It would pass as quickly as it came, he knew.

As the new draft of vodka went down his throat, he heard the familiar faint sounds of grains of wind-blown sand striking the glass of his window and the sides of the barracks. What a contrast to the air base in the Urals, he thought. There it was always cold, and the sky always clear, translucent as the vodka in his glass.

The reassigned pilot learned that he had been selected to train on the newest war plane in the Soviet inventory. This was the Berkut MFI. The Berkut was a stealth fighter aircraft. It had been developed as part of the Soviet air force's advanced tactical fighter program.

The ATF program was necessary to design, test,

and field new first-line fighter aircraft to replace the obsolescent Sukhois and MiGs that were currently the mainstay of Soviet air forces.

Already by the first decade of the twenty-first century, Western air forces had placed fighters into service whose performance envelopes were far superior to what the Soviets had available. The Americans had fielded their F-22 Raptor and F-35 Joint Strike Fighter.

The development of the latter was especially ominous. The JSF had taken a leaf from Russian design philosophy and had been built with common off-the-shelf components and modular technologies to make it cheap to build and inexpensive to maintain. As part of the JSF program, the U.S. was also making variants available to its Western allies. These variants were to be produced indigenously under contract.

What this meant was that the Joint Strike Fighter, in addition to native programs like Eurofighter and the French Rafale, could in a short time make the best that the Soviets flew obsolete. The Soviets had to do something. Strapped for funds as they were, it was a choice of developing an advanced tactical fighter of their own that was agile, stealthy, and long-ranged, or they'd have no credible defense against Western war planes.

The Berkut was the result of the program.

Petrovich thought it a plane as beautiful as it was unconventional in design. When he first climbed into the cockpit he was also impressed by the plane's advanced avionics suite.

Four multimode display consoles augmented a head-up display, or HUD, that was equally advanced. The throttle system had been also redesigned to match or exceed Western aircraft. It was a HOTAS system that was light-years beyond the old-fashioned "pickle stick" used by virtually all last-generation fighters, whether they were MiGs or F-16s. The HOTAS stick felt comfortable to the hand, and its control surfaces were as intuitive as using a computer mouse.

The representative of the Sovitel Design Bureau that had won the Soviet ATF competition was pleased by the pilot's admiration of the plane. On this first day with the new fighter plane, he walked Petrovich through the new system of controlling the aircraft and operating its weapons.

"That will be all, for the present," the technician told Petrovich when they'd finished the tour. "Before you next climb into the cockpit, there will be simulator training, and a great deal of it. We can't have you crashing this expensive piece of hardware on the first flight, now can we?"

Petrovich set down the glass. The dust storm had passed as expected and had lasted all of six or seven minutes. Now the desert landscape was still again. The clear blue sky was as translucent as before the storm's arrival.

He remembered how he had been challenged in the weeks-long simulator runs. Finally he had flown. It was a good first flight, and Petrovich's attention during the qual-sim trials had paid off. He was conscious that he was being watched critically, so that it was with relief that he was congratulated on this first test flight.

He sensed that a watershed had been reached, that a critical line had been crossed. He sensed they would have washed him out had they not been satisfied. He was in.

Petrovich recalled how he was pleased at having been chosen for another reason. The plane, he saw, was his ticket out of this new twenty-first-century Soviet society. After the brief fling with capitalism had failed to produce lasting reforms, the hard-liners had come to power. Soviet Premier Boris Timoshenko's coup had sealed the fate of the Rodina. The motherland was soon again under hard-line communist rule.

There could never be another Iron Curtain, though. Technologies of communication had made such a thing more impossible to enforce than it had been during the time of Stalin and the Oligarchs that followed from Kruschev to Yeltsin. By allowing and even encouraging such connections with the world at large, the reformer Putin had made lasting and permanent changes.

Petrovich was part of a restive society. He did not want to live under a new communist regime, because this regime was more truly Stalinist than communist, with Timoshenko as Russia's new Stalin. At the controls of the Berkut, Petrovich realized that fate had handed him the means of escape. All he had to do was to defect with his plane. The West would welcome him with this rare and special gift.

Petrovich didn't see such an act as treason. He was well aware as a matter of course that if he was found out, he would be put to death. He was also well aware that even once he'd defected he would be placed under a sentence of death by *mokri dela.* This meant that a wet-operations squad would have his name on their list, and if they found him a target of opportunity some day, then his number would be up.

He was willing to take these risks. Escape was that important to Petrovich. It was worth these risks and many more besides. Nevertheless, things had changed. He had hoped to spirit the plane away during one of the training runs. The sudden reassignment from the Urals to Libya made his spirits lift, for here it seemed that fate had again played its hand in Petrovich's favor.

From Libya it was a little under six hundred miles to the Greek island of Crete, which housed an American air base at Souda Bay. This destination was well within the plane's operational range. Once in flight, Petrovich could transmit on international frequencies. It was clear that the Russians had vetted him as thoroughly as they'd done to forestall the threat of a pilot defecting with this advanced plane. Once in flight, conventional aircraft would have little chance of intercepting him.

Then had come the news of a military confrontation in the Med. And now this—the fact that he and his wingman were to attack the fleet and attempt to sink it with nuclear missile strikes. This changed matters drastically. A peacetime defection was one thing. But a hot defection in wartime was quite another.

Petrovich was caught between the rock and the hard place. Should he try to defect, he might be shot down. Should he carry out his orders, he would commit an insane act destined to create shock waves that would engulf and crush him one way or the other.

He poured himself another glass of vodka as the sky darkened and another dust storm blew in across the desolate surface of the wasteland beyond his barracks window.

book three:

An Undeclared War

Previously, we were postured to defend against a state projecting force across great distances, and we built extensive capabilities to provide us early warning and tools to deter aggression. But the potential destructiveness of an attack of the type we suffered on 9/11 means that we are no longer afforded an opportunity to determine an "appropriate response" nor make a clear determination of when decisive action is too little or too late.

—Defense Official/Pentagon Press Briefing.

chapter *twelve*

Colonel David Saxon nodded to the Marine sentry posted outside the gray metal door and keyed his access code into the cypher lock. The faint clicking of cylinders disengaging and the message ACCESS APPROVED followed this action. Saxon cranked the door handle and went inside.

Beyond the door was Marine Force One's operational nerve center at the Pentagon. The MF-1 command center was a suite of metal-clad rooms secure to electronic penetration and linked into a global network of surveillance, reconnaissance, and analysis that girdled the planet. Real-time and near–real-time intel of every kind flowed from manifold digital sensors and human intelligence resources from points scattered the length and breadth of the globe and from the edges of near-space.

Saxon had been mired at the Pentagon doing staff work for the last several months, but at least he was still MF-1's commander. It could have been far worse. The attacks by Al Qadr in the continental United States that had embroiled Marine Force One in the most devastating terrorist action in the nation's history had left many wounds in its aftermath.

Al Qadr had struck with savage disregard for human life. Terrorist cells in the U.S. had staged assaults on targets in all civilian and political sectors. On what later became known as Strike Day, the terror nexus staged its most ambitious attack. This was a bid to take over the northeastern section of Washington D.C. known as the Federal Triangle.

Located within this part of the District was not only the Supreme Court building and Smithsonian, but also the Capitol. Saxon and Marine Force One had narrowly averted the consolidation of a takeover by Al Qadr of the Capitol while Congress was in session. The terrorist plan had called for the execution of senators and congressmen followed by the destruction of the Capitol building itself. Nearly simultaneous with this would have been the assassination of the president in the White House.

Had it all taken place as planned, the action would have dealt America a mortal blow from which it might not ever have recovered. Even so, the terror attacks had produced lasting shock waves that were still rippling and booming across the American landscape.

Part of the after-attack fallout had been a plethora of new plans for restructuring U.S. military forces. Those at the Pentagon who were opposed to Marine Force One had slipped their own pieces of machination into these plans. The Navy was eager to disband MF-1 and absorb what was left of the brigade into the SEALs. The USMCs go-anywhere, do-anything special forces brigade posed a threat to those in the USN who chafed at roles for the Marines that threatened some of their most cherished programs.

Saxon had fought tooth and nail to avoid reassignment to staff work at the Pentagon, but he was foredoomed to fly a desk at the Puzzle Palace for awhile. Saxon was due to rotate to staff work, as most officers did at least once during their careers. Fortunately, his mentor, and Marine Force One's godfather, General Patient K. Kullimore had pulled the necessary strings to ensure that Saxon spent the absolute minimum of time away from his field command.

Patient K. knew that MF-1 depended on their commander to hold the force together. Saxon was critical to MF-1's continued existence, let alone its continued success as a premier fighting unit. He was the force that drove the brigade. Ultimately, Saxon would turn over command to a new honcho, but this was still years away. Patient K. would retire, too. But not before he molded Force One into a special military formation with a permanent place in the nation's order of battle, one in as little danger of being disbanded as the Rangers, Delta, or the SEALs.

Saxon strode through a series of corridors, making his way into the inner reaches of the MF-1 command center. Once past another cypher-locked door he found himself in a cathedral-sized double-tiered crisis center. The battle cab's lower level, referred to as the bullpit, was sunk about a half-story below the upper gallery level.

In the bullpit were clusters of modular workstations and screened-off areas. Individuals or groups could work in private while monitoring the array of large, flat-panel display screens that were mounted on the bullpit's walls.

In the upper, or gallery, level of the two-tier operations center, seats were arranged in a horseshoe pattern and took up the middle and rear while the immediate front of the enclosure was occupied by command chairs and workstations with monitors. These stations were to be used in time of extreme crisis by Marine Force One brass.

This was such a time of crisis, and Saxon took the central command chair in front of a workstation that was all fired up, tied into the network, and ready for Saxon's passcode.

On the screen in front of him he was able to call up data from a variety of disparate sources, including a global network of supercomputers and real-time reports from the SPINTCOM and CRITICOM defense information channels. From his vantage point in the gallery, Saxon also had an unobstructed view of the four large flat-panel "god" screens on the wall beyond the rails of the battle cab's second tier and could monitor activity in the pit below.

"Status report," Saxon requested.

His exec in charge of South and Central American operations was down in the pit. His face showed up in a window of the colored rectangle that seemed to hover in the darkness in front of Saxon's command chair.

"Operations in cross-border areas of Colombia,

Ecuador, and Brazil are continuing. Sectors Blue and Gold are key operational areas, sir. As you know, they command the valley systems that stretch from Cinquentas, in the south of Colombia, into northern Brazil. Blue is secure. Gold is still contested."

Saxon acknowledged the report from the pit. He keyed video imagery onto the large flat-panel god screen in the center of the opposite wall of the battle cab. An Improved Crystal PHOTINT satellite had been jockeyed over this and other operational areas around the world to provide overhead real-time data to U.S. forces.

Saxon was one of the privileged few—whose number included members of the NSA, CIA, and Pentagon spy agencies such as DIA—to have unlimited access to the intel. He was also aware that at other key ops centers—the list was a short one—scattered throughout the U.S., others in the loop with the right clearances and the right needs-to-know were also looking at the same data.

The colonel leaned back in the formfitting command chair as he called for situation reports from the regions in which Force One was currently conducting operations. He poured water from a carafe into a glass and drank it. It was designer water, but without a label on the bottle you couldn't tell the difference, and it was a real glass instead of a plastic one, so he had no complaints.

One by one the sitreps came in. First from the cross-border region of Amazonia, then from the groups of islands scattered across the Philippine, South China, and Celebes Seas, next from the Gulf of Sirte bordering the southwestern Med, and the arid sand deserts hundreds of miles behind the Libyan littoral zone.

Finally, there came reports from yet a new regional trouble spot. It was one that had connections to at least one of the others Saxon had been monitoring. The new trouble spot was found in the southern reaches of the Eurasian land mass. It was in a region of flat, arid steppes that began at the point where the Caucasus mountain range petered out into a rugged carpet of weathered foothills, and where Europe became Asia.

Here, in a region known as Nagorno-Karabakh, part of Azerbaijan, there were disturbing movements of troops and war machinery that seemed to be positioning themselves for coming battle. There had already been fighting in this vicinity for decades, between Azerbaijan, whose natives were known as Azeris, and Albanians to the north.

The fighting was ostensibly over ancient tribal

lands but really about what was to be found under those lands—and that something was oil, lakes of it, rivers of it. The region of Nagorno-Karabakh contained some of the richest oil reserves in the Black Sea region, and as such, the land was a prize of incalculable worth to whoever could tap into it.

This time, unlike in the past, the troops massing for attack were Russian, and the neo-Sovs were being augmented by sizable contingents of Libyan troops. Al-Sharq had honored his treaties with the Kremlin. Tripoli had sent two divisions of combat troops to fight alongside the neo-Soviets.

It was obvious that such an opposing force would have little trouble in overwhelming Azeri forces and seizing the petroleum-rich region without much trouble. At least this would be true in a political vacuum, which, Saxon realized all too well, wasn't the way it would work.

Saxon was well aware, as he studied the intel in front of him, that there would be other powers who would rush in to fill the vacuum and potentially clash like titans.

Iran was one of them. Tehran was carefully watching events unfolding on its northern tier. And, Iran had territorial claims on Azerbaijan.

The European Union also had energy interests and

treaties with players in the region, including Bulgaria and Albania, and they, too, were poised to take defensive action.

Finally, there was the United States, which not only might support its NATO allies but also had its own energy interests to protect—a major new oil pipeline ran up from the region into Turkey, where the oil was pumped aboard supertankers for the cross-Atlantic trip to East Coast refineries.

Saxon had seen enough. He closed the map and database displays and opened a word processor window, then he began preparing a CRITIC-coded brief to the National Security Council and to the office of the Joint Chiefs. He believed that Marine Force One had a role to play in whatever military engagements might result from these new turns of events. Saxon was determined that Force One play its part in the regional conflict he was certain was on the way.

The president didn't look very well. His face was pale. He studied the ball on the putting green in front of him and prepared to take a swing. But his concentration wasn't there anymore. And there was that faint pain up and down his right leg.

Sciatica, the doctors at Bethesda had called it,

when he'd been worked up for that hellish week after the assassination attempt by the Mahdi's agent in the Secret Service. A nerve had flared up, a very long one that ran like a train track up along one side of his body. He'd be okay, they'd assured him. It would take a while, but he'd be all right eventually. Still, it was going on seven months since the terrorist attack called Strike Day, and President Travis Claymore wasn't feeling anything like all right yet.

Claymore still recalled the moment when he'd found himself staring down the barrel of a gun. The shock was compounded by the fact that it was his most-trusted Secret Service protector who had drawn the weapon and was a moment away from pulling its trigger to send a nine-millimeter round boring into the president's head. At pointblank range, he could hardly have missed and would have drilled the nation's chief executive, if not for the bravery of a short-haul trucker named Lomax, who'd thrown himself at the would-be assassin and grappled him to the carpet.

The occasion had been an awards ceremony in the Oval Office. Claymore was to decorate both the civilian hero of the Pittsburgh Oil Riots, who had saved a man from a blood-crazed lynch mob, and the members of the Marines special warfare brigade, Marine Force One. The members included their commandant, General Kullimore, and the commander of Force One, Lieutenant Colonel David Saxon.

Unfortunately, there were worse shocks yet to come. Hardly had the president been returned to a standing position when breaking national news reports came pouring in about an attack on the Capitol, and from the Al Jazeera news network abroad, concerning attacks on the carrier *Eisenhower* as it steamed through the Gulf of Suez from the Mediterranean into the Red Sea.

The attacks on the carrier and the ships surrounding it were made by kamikaze-style pilots who had flown air-launched Tomahawk cruise missiles that had been specially modified to carry human pilots for short distances to a target on suicide missions.

Intelligence later indicated that the Libyan dictator Al-Sharq, acting in conjunction with the fanatic despot who had taken over leadership of Iraq following the ill-fated U.S. occupation, had used the missiles salvaged from a downed B-1 Lancer bomber lost over the southern reaches of the Saudi desert during air-to-air refueling.

The president still recalled the horror of the carnage that those high-explosive strikes had wreaked on the *Eisenhower*. The damage had been immense. The carrier had burst into flames and, with a vast hole in its starboard side, had began to take on water faster than the ship's bilge pumps to could clear it.

Had the *Eisenhower* not been only a short distance from docking facilities at Port Safaga, Egypt, where it put in for repairs, it might have gone straight to the bottom. Which, of course, had been the intent of the strike all along.

The plan had been to block the Gulf of Suez to shipping, a move that would have placed a stranglehold on much of the petroleum shipments to Western nations, including the United States. This, in conjunction with scattered attacks on the global petroleum infrastructure, including oil tanker convoys in the United States and the enormous supertanker loading facility at Rotterdam, the Netherlands, would have surely resulted in an oil shock many orders of magnitude worse than the one OPEC had caused during the Carter presidency.

In the aftermath of such an oil shock, coupled with the assassination of the president in the Oval Office, the heart of the White House itself, and the takeover of the Capitol building with the resulting humiliation and execution of high-profile political hostages—senators and members of Congress would be shown with guns to their heads and knives at their throats before having those heads chopped off and throats sliced open—the nation would likely have been sent reeling from a series of blows from which it could never again recover its equilibrium.

That is what those terrible global disasters—collectively known as Strike Day—had been all about. Devastating blows struck at carefully calculated pressure points. Savage attacks coordinated to produce the maximum in physical, economic, and psychological damage to the U.S. and its allies in the West and Middle East. A symphonic masterpiece of terror conceived and staged by the shadowy figure called the Mahdi, whose whereabouts were presently unknown, but who was certainly still at large.

The president tried to force these distracting thoughts from his mind as he again concentrated on what should be the simple act of smacking the head of the golf club in his hands crisply against the side of the ball, and sending that ball arcing across the putting green to hopefully land in the number-three hole. He continued to find that performing this supposedly simple act was not an easy thing to do.

President Claymore would have preferred to have been behind his desk in the Oval Office grappling with fresh matters of state and new crises that had come up since Strike Day. The resurgent Soviets and the terrorist nexus were on the move around the world, and U.S. forces were at the moment engaged in violent regional confrontations in an effort to stem the red tide.

Lately, it seemed as though the nation had entered into a perpetual state of war with a hydra-headed enemy. You lopped off one head and two others sprang up elsewhere in the world to replace the one you'd just cut off. But the U.S. had to prevail. There was no other alternative to the chaos that would ensue if the other side won. The doctors at Bethesda and the shrinks at Camp David who had counseled him to take some time off to recover his equilibrium were wrong, the president now realized. His place was in Washington, not the putting green.

"Damn the bastards," he shouted, not certain if he meant his doctors, the nation's enemies, or both, and swung at the ball. It was a near-perfect stroke. The ball took off on a beautiful high arc across the green that brought it within an inch or two of the hole, then it rolled the rest of the way and dropped obligingly inside.

The president handed his club to an aide and climbed onto the golf cart. He told his driver to get him the hell out of there and back to where he belonged.

Then a strange thing happened. The president realized that for the first time in months he was smiling.

chapter *thirteen*

The *King Albert III* was now cruising through the waters of the mid-Atlantic some three hundred nautical miles southeast of the Bermuda islands. The weather was still mild, but the seas were colder here than in the subtropical reaches of the waters from which the liner had departed.

The seas were far deeper here, too; sonar soundings from the bridge gave readings varying from twenty-five to thirty thousand feet between the ship's keel and the bottom, and many an ancient wreck littered the seabed in these waters, the casualties of the Spanish conquest of the Americas and the Indies.

It was night, clear and dark because the moon was no more than a faint sliver of white perched like a small sail above the scudding clouds pushed along the horizon line by gentle trade winds. The seas were calm, and the radar consoles on the ocean liner's bridge showed nothing of any consequence either lying athwart its line of sail or moving toward it with the threat of collision.

From out on these calm, silent seas, to distances of scores of miles in any direction, the lights of the great ocean liner could be visible, shining like beacons in the darkness. The churning of her enormous screws could also be heard as a dull rumbling in the air while the strands of melody, snatches of conversation, or the burst of occasional laughter broke the stillness from time to time.

These were the hours before dawn, and on the bridge the night shift stood its watch. The men on the bridge monitored the instrumentation panels that linked the bridge to sensors onboard and to distant ground stations and satellites in orbit. Those indicators of danger all read in the negative, and the night watch had no cause to be alarmed.

Panic would set in after the captain was discovered lying on the floor of his quarters with the back of his head blown away by his own hand, but by then it would be far too late.

The hull of the boat had been painted—coated was a better word—in a matte black compound that had a rubbery quality to it. The thick coating was compounded by a mainland Chinese firm specializing in low-cost stealth technologies.

There were many such firms around the world, firms that offered both stealth and counterstealth solutions to governments and criminal cartels with the right connections and pockets deep enough to pay for the expertise.

The firm's clients found the cost to be high but not excessive, given the protections and advantages it afforded. Tonight, as the boat neared its objective, the results would be well worth the expense.

In the bowels of the ocean liner others were far busier than the night watch on the bridge four stories above. These knew what awaited the day shift in the captain's quarters. They knew because the captain was to have been assassinated by them before the next rising of the sun.

They knew because when the ninjas came, the

black-clad stealth warriors stalking through the silent companionways to find the captain and kill him in the night, and who effortlessly defeated the locking mechanism of the door, they found that the captain had already saved them the trouble. The ninjas said nothing, touched nothing, disturbed nothing. They merely glanced at one another through the eye-slits of their tactical masks and left the room, locking the door behind them.

Now the ninjas set about carrying out the second phase of the predawn activities. In the huge warehouse-sized cargo hold of the ship were stashed shipping containers concealing a cache of arms and explosives that had made it through the tight security net surrounding the ship.

The security net began at the point of origin and included anything taken aboard the liner. Crew were thoroughly checked, passengers were discreetly vetted, baggage was subjected to intensive X-ray, metal detector, and chemical-agent sniffer scanning. The system was designed to insure that nothing in any way hazardous to the safety of the ship or its passengers came aboard.

This chain, like many a chain, had a weak link, however. Computers logged pertinent data concerning cargo manifests, personnel records, and personal information on passengers, such as passport numbers. These same computers, if compromised, could just as easily be made to show false information on all of these things as surely as they normally showed the facts they had originally been programmed to display.

Computer security was high, but hackers know that the human link in the chain can sometimes be the weak link. Data can be tricked or coerced from people that no machine can be forced to give up. Hackers call this "social engineering." The captain of the ocean liner had been socially engineered. Blackmail had been the tool that had been used to unscrew his conscience and make him do certain things he'd not have otherwise done.

The captain had operator privileges on the computer system—he had security passcodes restricted to a chosen few. He could make the computer lie about certain things. Not many things, because his privileges were not as extensive as those held by the shipping company's CEO and board of directors, but extensive enough to permit him to give certain unauthorized parties access to the system.

The captain wasn't told much, in fact he wasn't told a great deal at all about why all this was being done, but he suspected what was going to happen and with whom he had been dealing. When the chance presented itself, the captain discreetly logged into the ship's computer system using his passcode. He immediately noticed a number of unauthorized changes to the ship's manifest, timetable, and route. Put together they spelled one thing, and this one thing was terror on the high seas.

It was later that same night that he put a bullet into his head.

Through the windows of the bridge, the sky appeared as black and flecked with stars as it had been throughout the night. The bridge clock announced that this was soon to change. It was approaching 0400 hours, and the sky would soon begin to lighten, the stars would fade, and the horizon line would become a glowing sliver at the edge of the sea.

Members of the night watch stretched and yawned. Some got up and walked around, exercising stiff and tired muscles. Lars Oscarborg, the liner's first mate, had gotten up to see if there was anything drinkable in the bridge drip-coffee-maker.

The third pot of the night had already been drunk

to the dregs, though, and Oscarborg walked away. He raised his arms above his head, linked his fingers, and cracked his knuckles, looking out through the night. He thought he began to see the horizon line, faintly limned against the stark blackness of the sky, but it was early still, and he figured he was probably imagining it.

Oscarborg was about to turn when he noticed something odd in the reflected overlay of the bridge on the surface of the window pane. There was a sudden movement behind him that was out of synch with normal activities on the bridge. Now discordant sounds were beginning to register on his consciousness. Sounds of scuffling. As he turned around he saw to his shock and surprise the masked figures enter through the access door. They were carrying snub-nosed compact automatic weapons.

Oscarborg spun on his heels as the attackers rushed the ship's night-watch personnel on the bridge. To his horror they fired at third mate Nick Collins. Collins fell to the deck. He twitched and lay still with a pumping red arterial wound in his neck. Oscarborg rushed to the third mate and crouched down beside him. One of the attackers smashed him across the side of his head with the metal stock of an automatic weapon.

He felt himself lose consciousness. He didn't hear himself moan or see himself sprawled near the third mate's corpse. Nor did he feel the steel tip of the combat boot that prodded him in the ribs.

Amidships, on the lower promenade deck, and aft of the last of the liner's starboard row of lifeboats, three masked figures stood in the cold wind off the Azores in the second hour before the onset of dawn. Two of the three worked security, keeping their eyes open for trouble and their compact auto-weapons ported at their hips.

The two working security patrolled the starboard deck while the third stood near the railing and looked out over the still-dark sea. All three wore night-vision headgear. The central figure used his night-seeing display to scan the slowly lightening horizon for the approach of the vessel that carried the boarding party they were expecting. He was the hawkeye.

After a time, the faint sound of specially baffled engines became faintly audible in the distance. The hawkeye would not have noticed the sound had he not been listening for it. Nor would he have become aware of the faint, barely perceptible shape of the approaching boat that was limned against the horizon by the faintest of visual traceries. It had been specially built for night operations, and the boat was highly stealthy to thermal and infrared imaging.

The coded flashes of an infrared strobe silently informed the hawkeye that boarding was imminent. Invisible to anyone not equipped with night-vision equipment, the flashes were clear and distinct in the view field of the head-mounted display worn by the hawkeye. The hawkeye raised his own compact strobe unit and clicked the button to send back the prearranged recognition code. Then he, too, took up his weapon and awaited the arrival of the boarding party.

The kitchen staff had standing orders to send up breakfast to the captain's quarters at 0430 hours every morning. The captain's orders never varied. He was to have a pot of hot black coffee, a half-carafe of grapefruit juice, two eggs sunny-side up, and bacon and rye toast, both extra crisp.

This order was dutifully filled by the ship's chef and passed on to one of the cabin boys who had just come on station to work the early shift. The cabin boy placed the order on a trolley, which he rolled into elevator number three.

The companionways were silent at this hour, and

he noticed the expected assortment of shoes outside cabin doors waiting to be picked up for shining and leftover trays from late-night dinners and snacks awaiting collection by the custodial staff. Absent were breakfast trays—these had not yet been delivered. The kitchen officially opened at 0730 hours, still some three hours away. Only the captain enjoyed the privilege of an early breakfast.

The cabin boy watched the lights of the six floors blink on and off as the elevator ascended the shaftway. The final light blinked, and its doors slid open. The cabin boy trundled the breakfast cart through the doors and out into the silent carpeted corridor. He wheeled it to the door of the captain's quarters and rapped twice.

Normally there would have been the faintest sound of footsteps behind the door, and then the captain would appear, thank him, and take the breakfast tray. This time there was silence. The cabin boy screwed up his face and rapped again. He thought he heard a faint sound coming from behind the door. He was about to knock again when the door opened.

His mind hardly had time to register the shock of seeing the black-suited figure in the black woolen mask with four slits for eyes, nose, and mouth, who stood in the doorway. The shock was cut short by the end of the cabin boy's life as two silenced heavy-caliber rounds spat from the bulbous suppresser on the muzzle of a semiautomatic pistol.

At pointblank range they ripped through his chest like hot knives through butter.

The stealthy boat was invisible no longer. Tiny by comparison as it bobbed in the waves and kept pace with the much larger ship, it was nonetheless there for all eyes to see. There were none to see it though, except possibly for early risers in their staterooms, but even they would have had a hard time noticing it in the darkness that came before the false dawn lit the sky.

The hawkeye had slung his weapon over his shoulder for the moment. He had been occupied during the last few minutes with a task that he had rehearsed prior to the mission. The motorized winch had been custom-manufactured to attach securely to the railing that encircled the lower promenade deck.

The hawkeye had secured the fastenings that attached the winch to the ship's railing. He then put the motorized hoist into reverse and dropped the climbing rope to the surface of the ocean below. As he peered down, his amplified night vision showed him the first of the boarding party grasping the line and placing his feet on the stirrups that depended from the end of the ultra-strong Kevlar-nylon cable.

There now came two sharp tugs on the line. The hawkeye reversed the polarity of the power switch, and the winch motor groaned as it strained to spool up the line against the weight of the man at the other end. Though it complained, the mechanism performed as flawlessly during this actual operation as it had in test trials conducted prior to the mission. The winch slowly pulled the figure from the boat along the porthole-studded wall of the immense vessel.

The first member of the boarding party to arrive onboard extended his hand as he was within two feet of the railing. The hawkeye helped haul him onto the deck.

"I trust everything is in order," the man said in a voice that brooked no argument.

The Evangelist was about to take charge, and his practice was to make sure everyone knew he was boss from the first moment to the last.

"All is in readiness, sir," the hawkeye answered

crisply in tones showing respect for a superior.

"Lower the winch," Evangelista ordered him next. "And hand me your weapon."

All over the immense surface area of the ocean liner, controlled chaos was taking place. On the upper deck, a pair of early morning joggers found themselves surprised by a masked figure toting a compact submachine gun who'd suddenly materialized in their path.

The couple, who were plumbing contractors from New York City, chose to ignore the menacing figure. The commando stepped aside while they began to round the corner of the stern of the vessel where the promenade deck made a U-shaped curve. The masked figure heard laughter and the sound of their comments. They clearly did not believe what they had seen, thinking it was some kind of prank. They seemed to be in another world, thought the gunman. But that was okay. He was about to send them there permanently.

Behind the mask, the figure's lips curled into a smile. He squeezed the trigger. The Spectre SMG, which was the type of weapon he cradled, was set on three-round-burst mode. The rounds were hollow-point dumdum types, named after a nineteenth-century British arsenal in an Indian city of the same name, and they fragmented on impact when striking bone and muscle.

The joggers shrieked as the burst of automatic fire chewed them up. Blood spurted from their bodies in hot red gouts. The masked shooter laughed and triggered another three-round burst at their heads as they toppled down. As they lay twitching on the blood-drenched deck, he shot them again.

"Stupid fuckers," he said as they died.

Elsewhere on the ocean liner similar acts were being committed. The killers had been given free reign to slaughter as many targets of opportunity as they could handle. Terror needed to be inflicted on as many as possible. There were hundreds of passengers onboard, and there would still be plenty left alive to use as hostages even after scores had been killed.

There was only one instance where the lives of passengers were to be spared. A crew of ninja gunmen was looking over the ship's computerized manifest at that moment to find out where they might be located and taken into custody.

These particular voyagers had been marked out for special treatment. The orders given the hit teams that had invaded the ship were to make absolutely certain that they were captured unharmed. The shooters could kill anyone else at their pleasure, but the fates of these two were matters for others to decide.

chapter *fourteen*

With the major hill towns commanding the key strategic valleys in the cross-border region of Amazonia now falling one by one into the hands of U.S. forces, combat operations in South America began to enter a new phase.

The insurgents no longer enjoyed strategically favorable positions. Their freedom of undetected and unfettered movement, key to success in guerilla warfare, was compromised in some sectors, severely restricted in others, and wholly absent in yet others under ever-tightening U.S. control.

In essence, the insurgents were now in the position

of fish in a barrel, with the walls encircling them becoming narrower all the time. As control was consolidated, the nature of the fighting was soon destined to change into a mop-up campaign rather than a contest between two opposing enemy armies, each enjoying certain advantages over the other.

But though one-sided, and with a final outcome that could be reasonably expected to result in U.S. victory, the battle that would follow could well turn bloody. Once hostile indigenous forces went to ground, they could effectively stage constant spoiling attacks on forces in control of the terrain, and if the pace of these attacks was kept up, they could have crushing effects on morale.

Such had been the case in Somalia and in Iraq, and long before that, in Indochina. The Evangelista rebels knew their history lessons as well as anyone else. They also held to the conventional wisdom that the United States would turn back from protracted conflict and large body counts. The strategy of the insurgents in Amazonia would now follow a predictable pattern.

As the tide of battle shifted with the new realities of war in the region, Marine Force One's role in the battle zone also changed. Elements of the MF-1 brigade were now regrouped into compact units of roughly company strength. These special detachments were given a new mission: to search out, locate, and then annihilate enemy formations still active and posing a threat to the force within the area of operations.

The detachments operated out of forward operational locations or were simply helo-dropped into the jungle at remote LZs that overhead surveillance—be it from aircraft flying RSTO or orbital assets of various kinds—had identified as harboring active or sizable insurgency forces.

Once at the LZ, the MF-1 detachment would be on its own for protracted periods of time. Anything could happen. And if it did, there would be no help. It was up to the forces in-country to pull their own chestnuts out of the fire if the action became hot.

The unit entering the lush jungle valley did so under tactically prudent conditions. The morning sun shone from an azimuth that did not put light directly into the eyes of the infantry. The moisture of fog-laden air circulated in undulating curtains of mist, but it did not hamper visibility and would quickly burn off.

The main inbound force had followed standard

procedure and sent out recon and security patrols. There were two of these patrols at squad strength, and they entered the valley from opposite corners. The patrols had not identified a great deal in the nature of a threat as they worked the terrain. They had stopped to reconnoiter and reported their preliminary findings to the main body of the force that was encamped some distance away.

"Thunder Seven to Ripper Zero."

"Roger. What's the deal?"

"I can report that this fucking valley ain't got no jolly green giant anywhere in it."

"That mean we can come in?"

"Not yet, compadre," said Sgt. Death, who was using a compact satphone, with encrypted comms, the size of a cell phone. "Want to check some more shit out first."

"Right. You let us know what the deal is, compadre. We're getting pimples on our butts sittin' here in the boonies."

"Any fuck-you lizards around?"

"Yeah, there goes one now—fuck you, fuck you, fuck you. You heard that, right?"

"Yep. Gonna break squelch now, compadre. Be back soon with the sitrep."

"Stay loose, faggot."

"Always do, faggot. Out."

Sgt. Death stowed the satphone in a quick-grab pouch on the load-bearing combat harness that held all kinds of goodies for specialist field work. These included mini-grenades and spare clips for the Spectre SMG that he wore in a breakaway rig across his chest.

The Spectre was secured by clip fasteners so it could just be ripped right off his fatigues and whipped into firing position real fast—MF-1 shooters practiced this feat so they would have the SMG out and throwing lead in under two seconds.

More spare clips for the bullpup Kalashnikov AKS-74s that Force One personnel ported instead of M-16s or M-4s, and other assorted gear including a personal GPS unit and government-issue scumbags to keep rifle barrels protected against the ravages of jungle warfare—among other things—were also handy.

The six-man, squad-strength patrol carried much other gear as well. The sergeant popped a stick of gum into his mouth and began to chew as he kept a weather eye out for signs of ambush, and another on what two other members of the squad were up to at the moment.

Once upon a time, a deep-penetration unit, like the LRRPs in 'Nam, might have relied on little else than that amalgam of hard-earned lessons and finely honed instincts collectively known as a "jungle mind" and a miscellany of gear pretty much limited to rifles, Claymores, and grenades, with F-4 air support or a helo gunship available on occasion. In those bygone days, specialist Marine and SEAL joint forces would hump the bush on search-and-destroy missions that took them deep in-country and generally far from any friendly forces that might come to their aid if they got caught in a jam.

Like other twenty-first-century combat forces, specialist force recon elements hived off the MF-1 brigade were equipped with advanced surveillance and reconnaissance gear that soldiers in previous wars didn't have available. These included unmanned aerial vehicles small and light enough to be packed in to wherever the hell it was that the Marines might need to go.

As the sergeant looked on, chewing his gum, two Marines were setting up for a micro-air vehicle launch. They were going to launch two MAVs in quick succession for a look around the area. The MAVs were two-stage heliprop affairs, one rotor on top for lift, and the other on the bottom for push and stability.

In the center was a sensitive video camera and thermal-imaging sensors, and behind these the components needed to transmit the intel that the MAV collected back to the squad and the high-capacity battery array needed to power the rotors and other onboard equipment.

It only took one Marine to set up the MAVs and get them ready for flight. The other Marine had broken out milspec hardened carrying modules that contained the ground tracking equipment. This was basically an antenna array that could be pointed at a dedicated Milstar satellite from which the MAV bounced its transmissions for over-the-horizon reception, and a government-issue laptop in a crush-proof metal casing that translated the transmissions into a form comprehensible to grunts on the ground.

By the time the sergeant's chewing gum had lost its flavor and he was ready to pop a fresh stick into his mouth, the first MAV was away and the second was about to follow it into the wild blue yonder. The micro-air vehicles were specially painted in a pattern and color scheme that would make them hard to see from the ground at their operational altitude of two thousand feet. Once they sailed up, they seemed to disappear to the mark-one human eyeball.

It wasn't long before the MAVs were paying off dividends. The valley system, which contained a river and numerous gullies, draws, and ravines, appeared through binoculars to be free of partisan forces from the patrol's position on the high ground that overlooked it. Seen from overhead though, the tactical picture began to change and a new and more dangerous reality began to emerge.

The unmanned recon clearly showed that there were hostiles encamped in the valley system. Quite a few of them in fact. The Evangelista rebels were holed up in there, but they had taken pains to make themselves as stealthy as possible.

The insurgent forces were hidden behind sophisticated camouflage screens of various kinds that were resistant to detection by visual means or even by thermal imaging. Computer processing of the raw data fed back by the two MAVs showed conclusively that enemy forces were encamped and active in the valley system.

While the Marine stationed at the laptop now began to plot these forces' exact locations on a sector map as the MAVs swept back and forth high over the terrain below, Sgt. Death had enough information to give his situation report to friendlies encamped in the jungle perimeter outside the mission area. Death had his satcom phone whipped out and was on the comms net to the leader of the main body of troops before the new piece of gum in his mouth had a chance to get soft.

"We found the jolly green giant, compadre," he

told the distant team leader when they'd established contact.

"Shoot me the intel."

"Preparing that now, amigo," Death replied. He looked over at the Marine at the keyboard who flashed him five fingers. "We'll have a sector map showing unfriendlies over to you in a couple of minutes. Should give you guys enough time to finish jerking off."

"We copy that, faggot."

Sgt. Death rogered that, signed off, and stowed his comms.

He popped yet another stick of fruit gum into his mouth and chewed, keeping a hawkeye out for trouble as the Marine sent the sector map to the troops in the field and pointed his MAVs back the way they'd come.

The sound of powerful turbofan engines screamed in Yevgeny Petrovich's ears. He felt the plane respond to the movements of his hand on the aircraft's HOTAS control stick at the moment he rotated the aircraft into a wheels-up position and translated off the ground.

The Berkut lept forward and gained altitude. Off to the side, Petrovich could see his wingman, Nikita

Malik, behind the Plexiglas-bubbled canopy of the second plane. The stealth fighters were about to fly their maiden combat sortie. The pilots both had their orders to attack the U.S. ships in the Gulf of Sirte. The internal weapons bays of both Berkuts carried the maximum load of offensive armaments.

Petrovich suppressed a shudder at the thought of the destructive firepower that he was about to unleash. A Giatsint missile armed with a nuclear warhead was part of the weaponload of his aircraft. There was only a single such nuclear weapon assigned the strike sortie, and his plane carried it.

The reason was obvious—only one such nuclear strike would be necessary. Should the stricken and badly damaged carrier force not immediately withdraw from the Gulf of Sirte, the two Berkuts could be refitted with additional weapons on their return and quickly redeployed for another sortie against the U.S. ships.

But Petrovich had no intention of carrying out the orders he had been given. He had not confided any of his concerns, plans, or reservations to his wingman. Malik was nothing but a vapid little party *aparatchik* who, Petrovich surmised, would not hesitate a moment to report him to the political action officer that had been sent to Libya by Moscow along with the other GRU cadre. Malik would in fact hasten to turn Petrovich in because he would believe it to be good for his career. Of this, Petrovich had little doubt.

Petrovich believed that in the ancient tradition of the military, it was a soldier's right and duty to disobey any order that he in good conscience could not carry out. This was one such order, and to disobey under such circumstances was not cowardice or mutiny or anything else except an example of the highest possibly bravery.

In the present circumstances, Petrovich was at a loss as to how he could manage to get away with circumventing his mission and still save his own life. He had mulled it over for hours prior to the commencement of the mission, wracking his brain as to how he could accomplish the union of two such direct opposites.

In the end, his mental gymnastics had been to no avail. The only way Petrovich saw that he could prevent himself from launching a nuclear strike against the U.S. carrier battlegroup was to either defect, ditch the plane into the sea, or simply return to base without launching the missile at all.

The first and last of the options he considered had the fact that Petrovich would still be alive at the end of the flight to recommend them. But as it was just as likely that Petrovich's days would be numbered after such a mutinous action, he considered that the middle course might save him a lot of time and trouble.

After all, why not just ditch the plane into the drink and get the whole damned business over with? It was at least quicker and more final an end than some of the other possibilities that presented themselves. Petrovich was almost sure to die a slower, more lingering and more painful death if the first and last possibilities didn't pan out just right, and it was more than likely that they wouldn't, he'd realized.

If Petrovich tried to defect, he would first have to signal the Americans that he was seeking asylum and to prepare for a landing of the plane at the nearest U.S. base, which was on the Greek island of Crete. By his computations, he would have enough fuel to cross the airspace between the coast of Libya and the U.S. base at Souda Bay in the southern Agean.

Should he pursue this option, it was more than likely that his wingman, Malik, would very soon receive orders of his own to shoot down the fleeing Berkut. That meant that Petrovich would have to shoot his fellow pilot down first or risk having to engage in an aerial game of hide-and-seek with the other Berkut.

Even if he proved the more capable air combat ace in the contest, the dogfighting would still slow him down long enough for other aircraft to reach standoff positions for missile strikes. He had no doubt that his own people, acting alone or in concert with the Libyans, would have no reservations whatever about blowing him and his wingman out of the skies if it meant saving the precious Berkuts from falling into Western hands.

On the other side of the coin, Petrovich could also claim that the nuclear missile he carried had misfired and could not be launched. He had no qualms about engaging the enemy with conventional weapons. This much he as a soldier in battle was prepared to undertake. Furthermore, a weapon misfire was not that uncommon a development in the Soviet air force.

Should he be able to damage the U.S. ships sufficiently with conventional strikes and cause enough damage that way, it was remotely possible that his superiors might suffer his insubordination. There were, he was certain, cooler heads in the GRU who would feel the same as he did about using a tactical nuclear weapon in a surprise attack on U.S. warships. Were international events, as a result of such a conventional use of the Berkut's firepower, to force the United States to turn tail and run from the Gulf of Sirte, then the resulting victory for Libya and her Soviet masters might well save his neck.

On the other hand, it might only postpone his

inevitable demise. The *Vlasti* in the Kremlin had a long collective memory, especially when it came to those who disobeyed orders. It would be entirely possible for Petrovich to be decorated as a hero and then, after a period spent glorying in adulation for his daring combat role in humbling the Americans, be quietly arrested and never again be seen in the light of day after that.

Stalin's era had witnessed a great deal of such disappearances, and Russia's new Stalin, Premier Timoshenko, had added twenty-first-century refinements to his predecessor's brutal techniques.

For the moment, the pilot of the lead Berkut continued to keep his plane on course. He would take whatever action was expedient when the moment of truth arrived.

That much he knew.

chapter *fifteen*

In the predawn twilight, most of the hundreds of passengers aboard the *King Albert III* were unaware of two facts that would soon be the cause of much concern to themselves and to other parties elsewhere in the world.

Fact one was that some of their fellow voyagers were no longer onboard the cruise vessel. They had been unfortunate enough to have run afoul of the commando assault force that had stormed the liner in the dead of night. These unlucky passengers had been killed on sight, then dumped overboard into the briny deep.

Fact two was that whether they were currently aware of it or not, every one of the passengers on-board the liner was now a prisoner of a group of cold-blooded killers who would stop at nothing to achieve their ends. The attackers would kill again, selecting victims at random whose bloody deaths would underscore their determination to achieve their objectives. But that would come later.

Now, in the few final hours that preceded the coming of dawn, there were many other tasks that needed doing.

In the operations center on the bridge of the ocean liner, the assault force was in complete control. Carrying cases and containerized baggage from the cargo hold that had been passed through security clearances were now being brought up via the main service elevator.

The secret cargo had been taken aboard with the help of the captain's interference with the ship's computer system, using his privileged passcodes. The bridge and surrounding spaces were now in the process of becoming the command center for the invasion force.

As the cargo cases were broken open, their contents were removed as quickly as possible. Commandos in paramilitary fatigues began to set up the miscellany of equipment that the cargo cases contained. This equipment ranged from sophisticated electronics and computer gear to weapon systems of various types.

In a short time the bridge of the ocean liner was becoming transformed into a high-tech military command center. Large flat-screen displays were placed on the walls while laptops and powerful workstations were networked to one another and also networked into the ship's onboard computer system.

The high-pitched scream of portable drills was heard all over the ship. Paramilitary technician squads, attired in the black commando jumpsuits worn by all of the attackers, were busily making a variety of modifications to the ship. These augmentations were for security purposes, command, control, and communications, and also for the deployment of defensive weapons systems.

Satellite dishes were being bolted onto the steel superstructures of the cruise liner. The dishes were of various sizes and configurations. Some would enable secure high-speed satcom transmissions to clandestine satellites and communications with distant command posts used by the Nexus and those who bankrolled it, such as the Kremlin and Tripoli.

Other satellite dishes would be used in conjunction with missile defense weapon systems that were also being installed onto the vessel. These dishes would be used for guidance and tracking, as well as for threat avoidance when conflict came with Western powers.

The keening whine of portable high-speed drills was intense in some places, accompanied by the sharp clatter of hammering and men swearing as they worked against the constraints of time and the friction of protesting machinery. Yet time was of the essence. The mission timetable had been carefully prepared, and each step toward the mission's end game calculated as rigorously as lines of code in a computer routine.

It was assumed that entities hostile to the invaders' undertaking would have received intel on the assault within between a matter of minutes and an hour, depending on such factors as the position and type of satellite surveillance or spy planes over the area of the south Atlantic where the hijacking had been carried out.

It was also assumed that once this fact was known, the Americans and their allies would all closely monitor the evolving stages of the hijacking and begin to deploy their military assets in order to stage a counterstrike on the ship.

Such reactions were expected and had to be factored into the mission timetable. The Americans, for example, had a number of forces specially trained and kept in readiness for hostage-rescue missions during terrorist actions at sea. The USN's SEALs were one of these units, and the USMC's specialist Force One was another and even more formidable threat to the undertaking, judging by this particular elite unit's past mission profiles.

For these reasons, small arms alone would not suffice to mount a credible defense of the ocean liner against the full spectrum of conceivable threats that might be encountered during the course of the mission. To bolster these low-level defenses, a sophisticated network of Falcon missile launchers was being installed at critical points at port, starboard, and at stern and bow.

In addition to the missiles, there were two CIWS-type Vulcan gun installations. The Vulcans could be swiveled around rapidly to bring fast, accurate fire to bear at high velocity on an incoming threat, such as a sea-skimming missile. With a boat full of hostages there was little possibility of such weapons being used against the cruise liner, but it paid to cover as many bases as possible.

As the gloaming of predawn twilight began to fade, and the eastern horizon changed from inky black to deep purple-blue, the efforts by the hijackers to arm the civilian liner continued at a fevered pace.

"Listen carefully."

The staccato sound of a burst of automatic submachine gun fire had cut through the din of voices in the grand ballroom only a moment before.

"Your lives may depend on it."

The hush that descended over the packed assemblage of passengers was so complete the sound of the proverbial drop of a pin could have been heard. They had been shepherded into the main ballroom from locations all around the ship. They had been dragged half-asleep from their cabins and staterooms. They had been frog-marched at the point of SMGs from early morning jogs. They had been manhandled from Jacuzzis and yanked from saunas. Some bore the swellings and wounds marking their initial resistance. Those injuries had been the result of the persuasion necessary to bring them to the ballroom.

Others had simply wandered in of their own accord. These were the sheep who were used to doing what others told them. Their faces and names were recorded on a special database for possible use later on. It might become necessary at some point to have hostages make video recordings pleading for mercy, begging the Americans not to attack, for example. The sheep among the passengers would be recruited for this purpose, if it came down to it. Others would make excellent spies and informants, valuable pipelines into any mutinies hatched by the captives as the hours and days of the takeover lengthened.

For the moment, all that mattered to Evangelista was that they were all here in one place, all here in front of him, his captive audience. It was a good feeling. As he stood on a platform raised atop the ballroom's concert stage that afforded him a bird's-eye view of the audience, he reveled in the sensation of having this large gathering at his total and complete command.

There had been no "Let's roll" bullshit here, and Evangelista knew these cowed passengers would present him with none in future. Certainly there might have otherwise been such displays of pointless heroics, but Evangelista's game plan had been carefully prepared to exclude this possibility as much as possible. The assault crews had separated out the potentially hostile elements of the passengers, first by combing the ship's manifest for anything that might indicate persons likely to give them any trouble, and then by weeding out potential troublemakers during the operation's roundup phase.

All those potential troublemakers were now cooling their heels in the floating prison into which a section of the ship's capacious cargo hold had been converted. As for the passengers who had been herded like submissive cattle into the main ballroom and faced him now, the presence of his armed commandos, positioned behind machine-gun emplacements, convinced Evangelista that the crowd would present no difficulties.

Evangelista tapped the microphone in front of him, assuring himself that the ballroom's public address system was on and properly functioning. Satisfied that it was, he launched into his speech to his captive audience.

"Ladies and gentlemen, please pay close attention," he began. "If you haven't noticed it already, this ship has been taken over by a group of very determined, very heavily armed, and very well-trained freedom fighters. Not only these men, but you yourselves are under my complete command."

Evangelista paused for a moment to give his words a chance to sink into their heads. As he paused he scanned the crowd. Their continued silence was encouraging. There wasn't so much as a stray cough to mar it. The fear in the eyes of most, if not all, of his captives was also encouraging. Knowing that they were terrified of him, because he held their filthy little lives in the palms of his hands, gave Evangelista a sudden rush of power.

He went on.

"Over you all, I hold the power of life and death. I can have any of you killed at the snap of my fingers. I have already given this order more than once. Several of your fellow passengers, those who've proven foolish enough to offer resistance to my men, have already been executed."

A murmur ran through the crowd at this revelation. Evangelista saw his armed guards react to the commotion by raising their weapons. They had been instructed to fire into the ceiling as a warning to silence should there be any outburst, and then to shoot into the crowd should this fail to cow them.

Evangelista decided that he would permit the sudden outburst just this once. He held up his hand as an order to his men to safe their fire.

"Even so, there is no great cause to be alarmed," he continued. "It's true you are my captives, yes. It's also true that I have no intention of doing you harm. You are, after all, more valuable to me alive than you are dead because I will have need of hostages before this mission is over. Then, too, the true enemies are the imperialists of the world, such as the Americans, that myself and my loyal freedom fighters are pledged to challenge. We recognize that most of you are merely dupes caught up in something that you have no direct part in and do not really even understand."

Evangelista paused again. Another murmur rose from the assemblage in the main ballroom. He permitted this, too. It was only natural that the frightened captives would whisper among themselves, or more accurately bleat and moo like the herded livestock they in fact were.

And as the slaughterhouse did with livestock, he, too, would manipulate them to his own purposes, direct them where he wanted them to go. In the end, they were all to die anyway. Of course, the less they knew of their impending mass destruction and the later they realized it, the better for his purposes.

"Now you will all return to your cabins. You will remain there as prisoners. You must understand clearly that under no circumstances are any of you allowed out of your cabins without my express permission. You will take your meals in carefully watched small groups to be made up of passengers floor by floor. There will be one meal a day from now on. Other than during these meal periods, anyone found anywhere in the ship without permission will be executed on sight. There will be no argument, no bargaining—only bullets and blood. I trust there are no further questions."

Without another word, Evangelista turned and stalked from the stage into what had formerly served as the dressing room area located off to one side. He had other business to attend to now. His men would make sure that the herd of docile captives was led to their pens in the meantime.

Some of the captives were anything but docile. Those from among the passenger manifest that Evangelista had ordered to be placed in the prisoner holding pens that had been set up below decks were largely male and largely angry. Some of them even had some military training.

"It's better if we move fast, before they have a chance to consolidate things."

Mal Foster was speaking in hushed tones. The whispering was necessary because for one prisoner to speak to another without permission was punishable by death, or so they'd been informed. Not that the captives in the ship's brig didn't take the threat seriously.

Many, if not most, had been brought there by force, and most of them still bore the sprains, pains, and wounds of their one-sided fights with the hijackers, all of whom were armed, while they were not. Some of the captives had seen fellow cruise passengers shot before their eyes and then summarily dumped overboard by the paramilitaries who'd taken control. They were well aware that the armed guards who made regular foot patrols of the cargo hold were not about to be played with. They were all clearly hard men who wouldn't hesitate to put a burst into any of the prisoners who gave them trouble.

It was now late at night, though, and the prisoners who had taken a chance to converse with one another had discovered that between the hours of approximately two and five in the morning there was some wiggle room for palaver. Whether or not this had anything to do with the guard detail posted during this stretch they didn't know, but the patrols were far more lax at these hours, and they could get away with talking in hushed tones if they were careful enough.

Charlie Sedgewick nodded at what Foster had told him. He, Foster, and a group of five other prisoners were huddled together in the center of one of the three large holding pens in which the malcontents and troublemakers were being kept. They had been chosen to be the group's mission-planning cell.

The word had been passed around to the other prisoners in the cell block—some of them were acting as hawkeyes, keeping watch for the approach of the late-night guard patrols. They would send a tap-code alarm—one, three, then two sharp raps that would be quickly passed on—in case an approaching guard detail was spotted.

"I agree. We've got to move fast. Because if we don't, the bastards' grip will strengthen, and any wiggle room we've got will evaporate."

"Right, and something else," Frank Medlo added, "I did some hostage negotiations work down in Colombia, which is where these guys are from, or at least where their honcho's from. Thing is, if they're doing this op South American style, which it might be, then the end game could be that we're all gonna die."

There were assents to this. Most of those in the brig knew that this sober read on their situation could well prove to be accurate.

"Right." It was Foster again. "It fits the scenario established on Nine-Eleven. Most terrorist takeovers since then have also been suicide missions. We have to act on the assumption that this one is no different than the rest. In which case we might be part of the biggest mass murder-suicide in history."

"Yeah, right. So what do you have in mind?" asked Sedgewick.

"I'll tell you," Foster replied.

And in tones even more hushed than the ones used before, he told them all.

The stateroom was one of the most lavishly appointed in the entire vessel. It was made up of a suite of rooms on the uppermost passenger deck that had all the features of a Park Avenue penthouse suite.

The occupants of the stateroom were anything but content at the moment, though. Two black-masked, black-fatigued, black-booted men carrying snub-nosed black submachine guns stood pointing their weapons at their heads, as the door opened and a newcomer strode purposefully inside.

"Mrs. Hunnicut and . . . what is your lover's name, I've forgotten."

"I'm Greg Rodham," said the man who had his arm slung around the weeping woman's shoulders. "And this is outrageous. Do you have any idea who she is?"

Evangelista smiled. Or, more accurately, he did something to his mouth that made it form the shape of a V and showed his teeth, but the impression was decidedly threatening instead of mirthful.

"You're absolutely right," he told Rodham. "I know exactly who this woman is. Or, to be more correct, who her VIP husband is."

"That's right. And her husband—estranged husband, actually—is the United States defense secretary, Warren Hunnicut. Heather is also a very important person and shouldn't be held here at gunpoint."

"I agree wholeheartedly," said Evangelista, using pleasant tones. "Now, my next question. Who, exactly, are you, and why should I keep you alive?"

Evangelista jerked his wrist and studied his watch. "You have fifteen, no, what the hell, thirty seconds, to justify your continued existence. If you can't do this to my complete satisfaction, I'll assume you have no justification and will immediately kill you."

"What? I mean—"

"Five seconds have just elapsed, Mr. Rodham, I suggest you begin defending your continued existence to me."

"Well, I, I mean, I take care of her. I mean, she needs me to do things for her. I'm her . . . her . . . partner."

"You're not convincing me yet, Mr. Rodham,

which is sad because you've only got fifteen seconds left."

"Heather, help me!"

Greg had completely lost his composure. Sweat stood out on his forehead in large, shiny beads.

"They'll kill me," he whined. "Heather! Please! These fuckers are serious."

He turned away from her, as he saw that she could not care less. Then he turned to Evangelista.

"Look, I . . . I don't want to die. Don't kill me. Please don't kill me. I know things about the bitch . . . I can tell you some shit that's—"

The sound the silenced Specter SMG made as it ejected a three-round-burst squarely into the gigolo's head at nearly pointblank range was little more than a subsonic belch.

The effects that the burst produced were far more spectacular, though.

The front of Rodham's handsome face all but disintegrated under the impact of multiple fragmenting rounds. A red mist of blood and bone appeared where his head had been, and a cascade of the pulverized matter splashed everything nearby, including Mrs. Hunnicut, who began screeching insanely as the headless corpse toppled over to land with a dull thump on the carpeted deck.

"Sorry, time's up," Evangelista said with a glance at his wristwatch.

He was almost cheerful as he gestured to his men to drag away Greg's corpse.

chapter *sixteen*

At first there had been nothing. No sign of activity, no indication of human habitation. There had only been the gleaming white strip of beach, and behind this the squat rocky bluffs that rose some twenty-five feet above the shore. The rest was mostly jungle, a rolling green carpet that undulated across the length and breadth of the island in the South China Sea along the chain of volcanic mountains that crisscrossed the place.

The mark-one human eyeball said one thing; surveillance intel based on both real-time photographic intelligence and synthetic aperture radar imagery from high-flying spy planes and orbital satellites told another story.

The island was a large one, part of the chain of rocky platforms in the warm southern seas belched up by oceanic volcanoes. Within the confines of its shores and deep in its jungle-covered hinterland were plenty of places to conceal guerilla armies, weapon installations, short-takeoff airfields, and clandestine operational bases.

These were precisely some of the nasty surprises that surveillance intel had shown to be present on the island. As a result, plans had been made to assault and take the island, and coalition ships, planes, and soldiers soon received orders to execute those plans.

Flame erupted. Explosions boomed. The world seemed to pivot on unseen hinges for the too-long beat of a soldier's hammering pulse. The air was blotted out by clouds of thick, choking black smoke. The bombardment from the sea was coordinated with air strikes ranging from F-35 JSFs using precision air-to-ground munitions, to advanced cruise missiles launched from submarines and ships from the carrier strike group situated offshore in the Sulu Sea.

These layered attacks were intended not only to prepare landing zones and other operational areas in-theater for the coming assault, but also to destroy or severely damage specific sites on the island believed to shelter Nexus command echelons, and thought to serve as storage locations for weapons of mass destruction.

Intelligence from CIA informants closely allied with the Nexus and run by their handlers under secure code-word cover also claimed that there was the possibility that the Mahdi himself might be in hiding in one of the cave complexes deep inland. If so, then the elusive mastermind of the global terrorist network that had committed some of the worst atrocities in human history might be trapped like a cornered rodent.

The news concerning the Mahdi was tempered by the awareness that it could very well be disinformation, not fact. Since the Mahdi's disappearance following the global terrorist actions on Strike Day, the terror chieftain had not been seen or heard from. This was the direct opposite of the Mahdi's tactics during the chain of terrorist attacks that had led up to Strike Day, when he was possibly the most visible person on the face of the planet.

For months during those upheavals, the Mahdi's face was practically unavoidable. The Mahdist forces had hacked into the Internet, hijacked TV and radio transmissions, used every technological means to deliver regular pronouncements from the Mahdi to the U.S. and European public. So intense were these attacks that they became known as "Islam spam." And then, as suddenly as he had appeared on the scene, the Mahdi dropped completely out of sight.

With the exception of the discovery by elements of Marine Force One of what might have been one of the rooms used by the Mahdi to make his media broadcasts in a remote cave in Yemen, there was no further sign of the Mahdi's presence. Still, in the absence of evidence conclusively proving his death, the most wanted man on the face of the earth was presumed by intelligence analysts to still be alive and at large.

As was the case with his predecessor, Osama bin Laden, it might be years before he was captured and brought to justice. In bin Laden's case, the terrorist chieftain managed to elude the internationally imposed death sentence by somehow swallowing cyanide after his sentencing following his months-long trial for genocide before the World Court tribunal in the Hague. Additional steps would be taken to prevent the Mahdi from following in bin Laden's footsteps if and when he was finally brought to ground.

For the moment, the phased, multilayered attacks from sea and air continued to assault the island, sending up incandescent mushroom clouds as powerful munitions exploded in shattering air and ground bursts. Sea-based observers could view the damage being done to enemy installations that surveillance intelligence had pinpointed earlier. Seen from shipboard through binoculars, the munitions strikes produced devastating results.

Other observers, in locations near or distant from the combat theater, were able to see and assess bomb damage at other levels. On computer display terminals in darkened underground command posts in the continental U.S.; on large, flat-panel god screens perched high on walls in code-numbered vaulted rooms in the Pentagon; and on TV monitors in combat information centers in American and British naval vessels anchored offshore of the island, remote real-time imagery of the battle was also being closely watched.

Robotic camera platforms had been parachuted into locations at various key points on the jungle-covered island. These robot spies and sentinels rolled and walked, or slithered and crawled, toward their objectives. There they observed and waited. Others bored into the earth, transmitting real-time imagery of the strikes' devastating consequences from the concealed cave complexes in which the Nexus hid its arms, troops, and war materiél.

As the op-tempo of the assault began to decrease and the peals of manmade thunder above the island dissolved into dying high-explosive echoes, the intelligence gained from those robotic spies would greatly speed up post-operational battle-damage assessments. Then the troops would go in.

As always, the Marines would be sent in first, and in their vanguard would be the specialist cadres of Marine Force One.

The formation of MF-1 troopers was at company strength. It was equipped for counterinsurgency warfare in jungle environments. Detachment Bravo had been issued its orders and given its objectives. Bravo's orders were to conduct active reconnaissance on a suspected Nexus encampment situated deep in the jungle.

This active recon—otherwise called a "recon by fire," or "fire recon," since it was implied that reconnaissance could give way to engagement with enemy forces in combat at any time during the mission—was to be undertaken by infantry, since standoff assets had not proved able to damage entrenched forces very much in this sector.

The Marines had gotten their orders while at Subic Bay naval base, which lies between Bataan and Zambales provinces on the main Philippine island of Luzon. Having been returned to the Philippine government decades before, Subic Bay was now again an operational U.S. base, leased back to the coalition with the onset of the global war against the Soviet-Nexus alliance.

The regional mini-wars, which, on Strike Day included the most savage attacks on the United States in American history, amounted in combination to a state of near-perpetual global warfare. Conventional and unconventional weapons were used in this planetary contest. It was fought on every conceivable battleground, from cyberspace to remote islands in sun-drenched tropical seas.

It was a savage kind of war, such as had never been fought before. Worse, it showed no sign of ever ending or even of ever being decisively won. Fighting the new enemy was like fighting a thousand-headed hydra which grew back two more heads for every one lopped off. Yet lopping them off one by one and two by two was the only option currently open to coalition forces.

This is very much what the Marines of Force One were being expected to do as they were shuttled to their landing zone deep in the jungle-covered mountain country in the interior of the large island in the Celebese Sea. Here was another head of the hydra, requiring another mission to lop it off; here was another battle fought against an enemy that seemed to be hidden in every corner of the globe. Whether or not it was a lost cause, the Marines were there to fight this battle, as well as the ones that followed.

The two Ospreys carrying Detachment Bravo and the unit's gear hovered above the mountaintop landing zone. The LZ was a natural clearing in the mountainous jungle that had been selected because of its suitability for the landing of troops and because of its proximity to the mission objective.

This objective, which lay approximately ten miles to the northeast, was a hill region that was believed to be honeycombed with a natural cavern complex. In addition to the cavern complex, intelligence analysts also believed there had been extensive construction of underground facilities nearby, as well as extensions and modifications made to the cave network.

The intel had been gathered in part from surveillance and in part from automated scans of global computer databases. The scans showed that largely Soviet, but also some European and Middle Eastern construction firms had been engaged during the previous two-year period to perform work on the island.

The records in the database referred to this work as "mineral and precious metals prospecting" and "logging activities," but on closer inspection the types of machinery that had been airdropped into the region weren't the kinds you'd normally expected to do those types of work.

The heavy machinery included mainly earth movers and precision drilling equipment, and the contractors' activities included far more blasting than logging or prospecting would have required. What seemed more than likely was that the true work being done on the island was the construction work of secure underground complexes.

The Marine Force One personnel were being deployed to check out the region for these suspected facilities prior to a major attack being carried out. This was for two principal reasons. The first reason was because a conventional attack on the suspected installations needed to have more precise, coordinated intelligence before it could be reasonably expected to succeed.

The coalition had a variety of earth-penetrating weapons at its disposal. These included conventional, non-nuclear munitions such as JDAM, and unconventional ATGMs such as the B61-11 tactical nuclear munition which could be air-deployed by B-1 Lancers to penetrate deep into underground bases and deliver a clean, low-yield nuclear strike far beneath the surface.

Both conventional and unconventional weapons had their drawbacks and limitations; as far as the nuclear option went, while the B61-11 could pop the base with a kiloton of explosive power, it was still a precision munition that needed to be deployed more like a scalpel than a sledgehammer. As powerful as the B61-11 might be, its use would need to be precisely calculated to produce the maximum in precision destruction.

There were political considerations in using a tactical nuke, too. Congress had mandated that the B61-11 earth-penetrator nuclear munition was to be deployed in combat only under circumstances where the use of conventional munitions could not conceivably enable U.S. forces to prevail or to meet the needs of the mission.

While all requests from CINCs in the field had to be piped up through the office of the Joint Chiefs of Staff at the Pentagon, it was understood tacitly that approval wouldn't be reasonably withheld if a regional CINC deemed it vital to the success of the war plan.

Just the same, while a CINC might have a good

expectation to get approval for a tactical nuclear strike against a deep underground target on his say-so, he could also be certain that he would get the okay for one, and only one, nuclear attack. Given this constraint, a theater CINC had to be extremely careful about how, when, under what operational conditions, and in pursuit of what precise tactical and strategic objectives, he would use his precious carte blanche to drop a nuke on a target.

That was why MF-1's Detachment Bravo was now beginning its trek into the jungles of the island. The team's leader, Sgt. Mainline, had been specially briefed on the exigencies of the mission. Mainline knew that use of the nuclear weapon would depend on the reconnaissance and surveillance intelligence that his troops would gather once they reached their objective.

Bravo would, in short, be the eyes, ears, and brain of the theater CINC, General Winrod Tedesco, and the general would put his request for deployment of the tactical nuke up the chain of command based almost solely on the field unit commander's recommendation. To nuke or not to nuke, that was the question. Task force Bravo's responsibility was not only to answer that question in the negative or affirmative, but to provide commanders with precise targeting coordinates for the most effective and tactically efficient use of the earth-penetrating nuclear munition.

It was, Sgt. Mainline knew, a weighty burden he carried on his muscular shoulders: if he miscalculated, the CINC would have a ready-made target at which to point the finger of blame. This was not a mission you wanted to mess up. Not if you wanted to retire on a full pension one day, which this particular NCO had every intention of doing.

As the troop-carrying Osprey rose straight up from the LZ, reached its translation altitude, and rotated its engine nacelles forward and down into convertiplane mode, then swung away to the west, the unit commander signaled to his troopers to move out. Eyes wary, the bullpup Krinov AK-74s that MF-1 used as standard mission kit—in place of the US M-series rifles—cradled and ready to fire at the first sign of trouble, task force Bravo filed out of the clearing and was soon swallowed by the dense foliage of the enveloping jungle.

Miles to the west, another combatant in the global battlespace was feeling the crushing weight of the orders he had received.

Inside the bubble cockpit canopy of the Berkut stealth fighter aircraft, Yevgeny Petrovich struggled to grasp the implications of his tactical instructions, and of the mission he was expected to carry out in pursuit of them.

The sealed orders had instructed him to stage a nuclear strike against the U.S. carrier battlegroup that was stationed off Libya's Mediterranean shoreline, well inside the "Zone of Death" proclaimed by the Libyan leader, between international waters and those claimed as national territory inside the confines of the Gulf of Sirte.

Against these apocalyptic orders, Petrovich gave thought to his own plans to defect to the West and bring his advanced tactical fighter with him as an insurance policy to guarantee his asylum. The Berkut was by far the most advanced stealth aircraft ever built by the Soviets, and in many ways was far more advanced than its counterparts flown by the West.

The Golden Eagle fighter departed radically from U.S. stealth technology in that it used an exotic field-effect generator system in addition to conventional form stealth design. The Berkut flew within an envelope of circulating ions that acted as a force field to deflect the probing main and side lobes of enemy search-and-track radars back and upward from its fuselage.

The Western design approach was to build the

aircraft so that surfaces on the fuselage themselves deflected, dissipated, and absorbed radar energies in such a way as to make the aircraft undetectable to radar. The Soviets had pioneered their unique active approach to making planes stealthy as opposed to the primarily passive stealth the Americans had built into their warplanes. The pilot had no doubt that the successful landing of the Berkut on American territory would be a gift horse that the U.S. would not dare look in the mouth.

Petrovich's plans called for his breaking off the mission profile once his aircraft flew far enough into the Gulf of Sirte to effectively place it beyond the lethality envelope of Libyan SAM installations situated along the coast. He knew that these were SAM 10 and SAM 11 missile launchers, adequate to defend against conventional fighter aircraft but near worthless against a stealthy fighter plane such as the one he now flew. Once over the gulf, Petrovich could be reasonably sure of immunity to even a lucky hit or lethal near-miss by the detonation of a SAM warhead near the plane.

At that point he would do two things: First he would break off from his attack vector with a wingover that would place him on a new northwest flight profile toward his objective. This objective was the U.S. air base at Souda Bay on the Greek island of

Crete. He knew he had more than enough fuel to reach the base.

Secondly, and more critically, Petrovich would immediately begin broadcasting his friendly intentions on all international emergency frequencies. He would try to inform the Americans that he was defecting, that he would make no hostile moves, and that his destination was Souda. If, and only if, he had to, he would take defensive action against his wingman. But he would give Nikita Malik fair warning by broadcasting his intentions just before he was about to break away. If Malik decided to pursue him after that, then his conscience would be clear.

The minutes ticked off as the moving map on the Berkut's central integrated multimode tactical display showed that the combat flight was only seconds from reaching its first waypoint. It was at this waypoint that Petrovich planned to turn and break for Souda Bay. After it was done, his actions would have become irrevocable; there would be no turning back following this move.

A series of dull electronic pings from the plane's inertial navigation system filled his headset as Petrovich and his wingman reached this first critical mission waypoint. The flight leader's mouth was dry as he keyed his comms to tell Nikita that he was about to defect and warn the wingman away. He steeled himself for what would come next and took the leap.

"Black Bear, this is Storm Giant."

"I read you."

"I have something to tell you. Listen carefully. I am about to—"

A loud series of high-low tones in his headset cut short the flight leader's words. The tones indicated that an urgent secure communication from flight control was to follow. It immediately did. The message was urgent and unexpected. The mission had been scrubbed. Both planes were ordered to immediately return to base. There had been no explanation, no warning. What was behind it all?

Petrovich's mind whirled like a precision machine unexpectedly thrown out of control. He had mere moments in which to reach a crucial decision. If he returned to base now, he had no way of knowing whether or not the order to scrub the mission somehow concerned his plans. Had his treachery been found out? Was the KGB waiting to arrest him, subject him to chemical debriefing, and then execute him? Or was it something else? Had the Libyan colonel gotten cold feet at the prospect of launching a nuclear attack on the world's strongest military power?

Whatever the reasons behind it, the announcement had left the flight leader stunned. He did not know which course of action was the correct one to now take. His hand froze on the aircraft's control stick. Off to his right, through the Berkut's Plexiglas-bubble canopy, he could already see his wingman begin to execute a sharp turn that would swing the plane back across Libyan airspace to its landing field inland.

Now, after moments of hesitation, Petrovich heard demands in his flight helmet headphones that he acknowledge the order to scrub the mission and return to base. Should he hesitate but a few moments more, he was sure there would be no choice left except to chance a run toward the West.

The moments of terrible indecision stretched into an eternity of self-doubt as the fighter plane streaked across the ocean.

chapter *seventeen*

The Shark of Tripoli nodded to his adjutant and turned away. He had just been informed that his order to the attack planes to abort their mission had been transmitted and acknowledged. He had dragged his feet on issuing the order, waiting until the last possible moment—almost until the planes had reached the point of no return—before ordering it sent.

The problem had kept him up all night. The new development that he had been informed of by the Soviets had come as a complete surprise to him. It had caught him totally unaware.

The Father Colonel had risen early, conducted his morning prayers, and then sat down at his desk to decide finally what course to take by the cold light of day. In the end he had issued the recall order, but now, in its wake, he was still unsure if he had done the correct thing.

It was, he succored himself, now in the hands of Allah, as were all things on heaven and on earth.

The black Cadillac limousine flying the flag of the secretary of defense sped across the 14th Street Bridge from the western shore of the Potomac. Its destination was 1600 Pennsylvania Avenue, on the other side of the bridge and through first Washington D.C.'s inner city area, then the more affluent Georgetown.

In the meantime the occupant of the back seat, Defense Secretary Warren Hunnicut, had a great deal to think about. Like the Libyan Father Colonel, he, too, was in a quandary, albeit concerning other matters. The clandestine communiqué from the hijacked cruise liner had settled any lingering doubts concerning his estranged wife's presence aboard the ship.

The communiqué had mentioned her by name. No—more than that, the communiqué from the terrorist hijackers had identified her as the SecDef 's wife. Video recorded images had followed, sent via the Internet from a location—probably in France—that the DIA, and what they called "OGA"—other government agencies—at the Puzzle Palace were still trying to pinpoint conclusively.

Well, good luck to that, the defense secretary thought as he glanced up from the paperwork perched on the upraised shank of his left knee where it lay crossed over his right—his customary riding position. They'd never find a valid IP address to link to the point of origin of those photos, he'd be willing to bet on that.

If he knew the forces they were dealing with—and the SecDef did, that was part of his job—then everything connected with the transmission, including the PDA or laptop that had originally held the image files, had been smashed to pieces and thrown down a convenient sewer. If it had indeed originated from Paris, then there were plenty of sewers there, he thought with as much hint of a smile as he could muster.

Nice to think your sense of humor's still partially functional, old buddy, the SecDef told himself. If that's still there, then maybe there's hope. Another part of his psyche immediately countered that with a "fat chance." Hunnicut silently said, "Shut up, Imp of the Perverse," and tried to force his mind to other matters, specifically the brief on the developing regional crises he'd give the president once he'd reached the Oval Office.

Apart from the hijacked cruise liner—more like a floating city than a ship, considering how many passengers were onboard, all of them hostages, too—there were several other global events that had escalated to the crisis stage.

One was occurring in the Gulf of Sirte, where the carrier *Clinton* and its strike group were locked in a Mexican standoff against the Libyans. With the Father Colonel holding the levers of power in Tripoli, all bets were off. The present Libyan maximum leader made his predecessor Qaddafi look as sober as a monk by comparison.

The other major developing crisis was what surveillance from space-based and aerial intelligence-gathering assets—backed up by reports from highly credible HUMINT sources—were showing to be an apparent surprise move by the Soviets to seize the rich oil fields of Nagorno-Karabakh in southern Azerbaijan.

The Libyans were involved here, too, having moved two divisions of their crack Jamahiriya Guard brigade troops into attack positions on the southwestern flank of the transcaucasus, while the Russians were massing at the opposite end of the region.

In a geostrategic extrapolation of almost Newtonian action and reaction, these moves had brought the big country in the middle of it all, Iran, into the picture as well. Having sent off strong demarches to Moscow, Tripoli, and even Western capitals, including Washington and London, for good measure, the Iranians had lately placed their forces on high alert. Breaking intelligence showed that at least two and maybe three divisions of Iranian mobile armored forces were now ready to deploy in battle.

Against what and whom was an open question, but it was a sure bet that when and if the Iranians moved—if not long before that—the EU's own Defense Force, which had in the last decade become more and more removed from NATO policy, would launch some form of unilateral action.

Apart from mutual defense treaties with several affected countries—including Azerbaijan's neighbors Bulgaria and Albania—the EU had been using the region's petroleum fields to satisfy its ever-increasing energy needs. The threat of these vital resources falling into Soviet hands would be enough to send some of America's closest and staunchest Western allies running amok in the Transcaucasus, and any calls for restraint from Washington be damned. The EU nations would retort that Washington had gone ahead and protected U.S. interests in

Iraq in '03 without asking anyone's permission, and now, over a decade later, the EU was going to do exactly the same, and damn the torpedoes.

Yes, it had to go down like that, thought the SecDef as the staff car sped across the 14th Street Bridge and onto the streets of the District beyond. But, by the same token, if it did go down that way, the five or six regional conflicts might well combine with a synergy that could result in total war within a matter of weeks.

Beyond this there was every possibility that somebody would lose their head and press a button, and then the crisis would escalate to the nuclear level. After that, two other significant factors could come into play.

The first was that the U.S. national missile defense shield, touted in the early years of the twenty-first century as a credible defense against nuclear missile attack, never worked as advertised. The second was that after the U.S. unilaterally tore up the SALT III treaty to pursue NMD on its own hook, the Soviets had reacted by pursuing a crash program to develop MIRVed and MARVed nuclear warheads so stealthy that nothing could detect them in an inbound trajectory, let alone stop them from striking most of their targets.

But shit, all that amounted to was the end of the

fucking world, thought the SecDef. On a personal level, once the bovine excrement concerning his wife's marital infidelities hit the whirling blades of the media, global apocalypse was nothing compared to what Hunnicut would have to suffer through.

As the limo rolled through the streets of the District, Hunnicut again tried to muster another smile.

This time, though, he found he couldn't pull off the trick a second time.

The mood in the Yellow Oval Room was somber. The large suite, less ornate and spacious than the State Dining Room or Blue Room, was nevertheless better suited to the full cabinet meeting than the more cramped confines of the Oval Office.

The president used his day-to-day work area in the West Wing for sessions with small working groups and personal meetings with visiting dignitaries and heads of state. Any presidential business that required larger working groups was generally deferred to one of the larger rooms such as the Yellow Oval Room, the Map Room, or the Treaty Room, which was located only a short walk down the hall from the president's bedroom and the White House Family Sitting Room.

The president almost never was a regular participant in meetings in the NSC crisis room in the White House subbasement. First, there was precedent—few other presidents attended meetings down there, except during times of extreme national emergency or global alert; the vice president was generally the highest-ranking member of the government found at NSC meetings. Secondly, the president was something of a claustrophobe and hated being cooped up in the windowless room with air that, despite it being scrubbed and purified by a filtration system, was to his mind always unbearably stuffy.

On the contrary, the president liked taking meetings in the Yellow Oval Room because this august chamber, which faced the South Lawn, received generous doses of morning sunlight that lasted well into the early afternoon. The place lifted his spirits, and this was a welcome respite from the many troubling cares of state with which he had to contend.

Unfortunately, this morning was not one of those days in which the sun chose to make an appearance and grace the meeting with its pleasant warmth and cheerful beams. A blanket of dull gray clouds covered the District.

The darkness of the day had necessitated that all the lights in the large chamber be turned on, something else the president, who preferred natural light, didn't favor. Since the subject of the meeting concerned a great many disturbing events, the president's mood was not a very positive one.

He'd kept glancing at his watch almost from the first. Now, midway through a scheduled two-hour meeting, he caught himself doing so again as National Security Advisor Ross Conejo wrapped up his delivery of an NSC analysis of the situation in the Gulf of Sirte.

"We believe, and I think the SecDef will back me on this, that a show of force would be advisable," Conejo said, glancing at Hunnicut's direction and receiving a faint nod in acknowledgment. "Despite considerable military aid from the neo-Sovs, our friend the Father Colonel is commander in chief of a force as hollow as the hole in the center of a doughnut. Tweak his nose and he'll do something dumb, like sending up some of his MiGs against our F-35s or Super Hornets."

"—Or he could do something smart, like launching an Exocet—or whatever the hell you call those Russian missiles that are exactly the same as the French ones—at one of our warships."

This outburst from Secretary of State Bernadette Hoffmeister caught the National Security Advisor short, eliciting a furious volley of eye blinks. If each of those blinks was a trigger-pull, thought the president, looking on, Conejo would have just blown Bernie to hell and smithereens.

The animosity between the two, one that had increased since the events of Strike Day over their conflicting interpretations and counsel, was well known.

"Our experts," Conejo pressed on, referring to the working group that had studied the crisis in the Med and included prestigious academics from some of the Beltway's best-known think tanks, "have drawn the conclusion that the Shark won't try this, but that even if he does, we have the means to destroy sea-skimming missiles well before they can strike one of our vessels."

Conejo again turned to Hunnicut as well as JCS Chairman General Buck Starkweather, who was seated next to him. "I'm sure that those here representing DOD will back me up on this."

Actually, neither the SecDef nor the CJCS were as confident as the NSA concerning the capabilities of shipboard antimissile defenses deployed on the vessels of the CBG in the Gulf of Sirte. They knew that the Soviets had invested a great deal of money on designing stealthy sea-skimming missiles, and that if the Father Colonel had some of the newest types in his arsenal—which was a possibility—then nobody could guarantee the safety of any vessel.

Hunnicut and Starkweather merely nodded; neither of them wanted to risk taking a firm position one way or the other.

State was quick to seize on the air of uncertainty that hung over the room.

"Seems like your friends won't play in your sandbox, Ross," she told Conejo. "Fact is, their silence speaks volumes. We all know that there's no sure defense against high-tech anti-ship missiles—nothing you can bank on, anyway."

Before Conejo could frame a reply, the president cut in.

"Let me be the one to decide what action we'll take in the Gulf of Sirte," he told Conejo. "I'll give you my decision by close of business today, barring any emergency developments, of course."

The president again checked his watch, thinking that this damn meeting was just crawling by this morning.

"What about the liner?" he asked.

"The *King Albert III* hijacking is being carefully monitored by all responsible agencies," replied the NSA.

Conejo went on, "The National Security Agency has been monitoring transmissions not only to and from the ship, but has also been collecting intel from other sources concerning the hijacking."

"A Libyan connection?" asked the president before Conejo could complete his assessment.

Conejo nodded.

"Analysis of the intel supports this view."

"Instead of asking for your further assessments about what to do, I'm going to surprise you all and suggest we make a strong show of force to retake the vessel. I've already been in touch with Prime Minister Atherton—as you're probably aware the ship is a British charter—and it's basically a joint decision between our two governments. Most of the passengers are American. We can't let the bastards produce a floating World Trade Center disaster."

"Mr. President," said the NSA, "as I informed you yesterday, there are—"

"I know, they've mined the ship, and there might even be a tactical nuke aboard," the president acknowledged. "Doesn't change my thinking on the matter one bit—nor the prime minister's, either. My question concerns not whether or not to go in and kick the terrorists' asses, but how to get the job done—and in a hurry."

A sudden silence hung over the Yellow Oval Room. Somebody was about to be put on the spot. "Buck," the president said to the CJCS. "You're it. What kind of specialist capability have we got that can handle this kind of a mission?"

"We have a number of specialist units that have been trained to handle an operation of this type, Mr. President. If what you're proposing is some form of joint mission with our colleagues in the U.K., then I can assure you that some of those units have in the past trained jointly with the SAS, SBS, and other special forces over there. I can meet with my people and report to you later today."

The president nodded and glanced at his watch. Fifteen minutes to go, he thought, and maybe he could cut the already too-long meeting short.

"I'll save you some paperwork, Buck," he told the CJCS. "I already have a unit in mind. The same one that took out the terrorists who'd taken control of the Capitol on Strike Day: Marine Force One. I understand that it's not only good to go, but it has the best specialist training in sea-air-land operations of precisely the type we're contemplating."

The CJCS looked away momentarily.

"Mr. President," Starkweather replied tentatively, looking his commander-in-chief nervously in the face. "I believe Marine Force One comprises some of the finest soldiers in the nation. But, Mr. President, the brigade's method of operation can sometimes be highly unorthodox. Under the circumstances, extreme caution should be the watchword. Sir, let me instead suggest the SEALs—"

"Buck, I wasn't asking, I was *telling*. Get me Marine Force One," he concluded. "And what was the name of that highly unorthodox unit's CO again?"

"Saxon, sir," said the CJCS, resignedly. "Lieutenant Colonel David Saxon."

The president nodded.

"Have Saxon report to me directly. Before close of business today."

The president glanced at his watch.

"That's it. Meeting's adjourned," he said. Then he turned and hurried from the room.

Approximately fifteen minutes later, a Marine in an A-uniform waiting for a slice of pizza at one of the fast-food kiosks in the Pentagon mall, heard his phone go off in his pocket. As he lifted the cell to his ear, he glanced at the number showing on its face. From experience he recognized the White House exchange directly behind the area code.

"Saxon," he said, and waited for the orders that he knew would follow.

DAVID ALEXANDER

MARINE FORCE ONE

A special detachment of the Marine Corps whose prowess in combat and specialized training sets them apart from the average grunt. They charge where others retreat, and succeed where others fail. They are the best America's got.

MARINE FORCE ONE

0-425-18152-9

As tensions continue to build between North and South Korea, Marine Force One is sent on a recon mission that reveals North Korea's plans to use chemical weapons against the south. But before they can report to H.Q., they are ambushed and overwhelmed by a relentless pursuit force.

MARINE FORCE ONE: STRIKE VECTOR

0-425-18307-6

In the deserts of Iraq, there's trouble under the blistering sun. Using an overland black-market route that stretches from Germany to Iraq, extremist forces have gathered materials to create a new weapon of devastation. It's a hybrid nuclear warhead that needs no missile—it can be fired from artillery. And it could cast a radioactive cloud over the entire Middle East.

MARINE FORCE ONE: RECON BY FIRE

0-425-18504-4

To find the leaders of a terrorist organization, Marine Force One heads to Yemen—but the terrorists have kidnapped an American Air Force Officer—and getting close to them puts his life in danger.

Available wherever books are sold or at
www.penguin.com

B532